"TIGHTLY PLOTTED,
CRISPLY CHARACTER-ED,
AND BLESSED WITH
MUFFIN/FREEMANTLE REPARTEE
AT ITS SHARPEST,
THIS IS A MINI-MARVEL
OF NEAT INTRIGUE."
The Kirkus Reviews

THE INSCRUTABLE
CHARLIE MUFFIN

The latest rollicking adventure
by the author of
CHARLIE M
and
HERE COMES CHARLIE M

THE
Inscrutable
Charlie Muffin

BRIAN FREEMANTLE

BALLANTINE BOOKS • NEW YORK

Copyright © 1979 by Innslodge Publications, Ltd.

Library of Congress Catalog Card Number: 78-20027

ISBN 0-345-28854-8

This edition published by arrangement with Doubleday & Co.,
Inc.

Manufactured in the United States of America

First Ballantine Books Edition: December 1981

for
Jonathan Clowes
With a feeling of great gratitude.

CHAPTER ONE

THE FIRE BOATS had been placed so that their sprays created a paper-chain of rainbows through which the *Pride of America* sailed when she left New York for the last time. Every vessel in the harbour set up a cacophany of farewell sirens and the streamers hung, like just-washed hair, over the ship's side and from Pier 90 and several other jetties by which she slowly passed.

Lights in the twin towers of the Trade Centre windows had been specially illuminated so that the message read "Farewell," to match the same word spelled out above the Manhattan skyline by the sky-writing plane which arced and circled above, its purple smoke streaming behind.

The waterside was jammed with people, and the Circle Line boats had arranged special ferry trips to remain alongside until the liner reached the Statue of Liberty, a vantage point crowded with more sightseers.

It was here that Mr. L. W. Lu called the major press conference on board the ship, to enable the film and television crews and journalists, who would not be remaining for the entire voyage to Hong Kong, to be conveniently airlifted back to La Guardia in helicopters waiting on the cleared observation deck.

There had been press flights from England and every major European country, and over two hundred people crowded into the dormer observation bar. Not since Onassis had there been a ship-owner more internationally known, so the press-kit was hardly necessary. But Lu was a consummate publicist. As each of the pressmen had entered the room, they had been handed a bulging file setting out the already familiar history of an orphan boy born into poverty who had risen from junior shipping office clerk to speculative investor on the Hong Kong stock market to tanker magnate, Asian oil millionaire, free enterprise entrepreneur, and benefactor of three fully supported orphanages and two hospitals.

He sat on a raised dais, the panoramic view from the ship behind him, patiently waiting amid the chaos that precedes any such gathering. By his side, as always, sat his son. There was a remarkable physical resemblance between the two men. The father was a Buddha-plump, benign-looking man, the harsh klieg lights of the cameras glistening against his polished face and silk suit and occasionally, when he extended his almost constant smile, picking up the gold in his teeth. John Lu was slightly thinner and, unlike his father, wore spectacles. He had no gold in his teeth, either, but it was difficult to establish because John Lu was a man who hardly ever smiled.

It was the younger man who stood first, holding out his hands for silence.

"My name is John Lu," he introduced. "I would like you to welcome my father, who wishes to begin this conference with a statement."

There was a surprising but isolated burst of applause from the Asian journalists present, and Lu smiled in appreciation. He didn't stand. He merely leant forward upon the table that had been set with microphones and radio equipment, tapped the mouthpiece to ensure he had selected the right amplifier, and said, in an ordinary conversational tone: "Thank you all for coming."

The microphone picked up the sibilant blur in his voice, but there was an immediate response, the room quietening within minutes. Lu's smile widened slightly at the command.

"There has been, I know, much speculation about my reasons for purchasing this still-magnificent liner ..." he began.

The man was very aware of the seating arrangements for the conference and spoke fractionally turned towards the section he knew to be occupied by Americans.

". . . I have always felt it a tragedy that a vessel like the *Pride of America*, still the holder of the Blue Riband for the fastest crossing of the Atlantic, should, because of a change in world travelling preference, be mothballed and lying, almost forgotten if not abandoned, off the coast of Virginia. . . ."

He paused. Imperceptibly, a glass of water appeared at his elbow from the attentive son. The Chinese sipped at it, smiling out at people he could no longer see because of the fierceness of the lights. He made almost an affectation of politeness.

"And so," he resumed, "I have found for it a function that will maintain the liner not only in its former glory, but put it to a purpose that will make it perhaps more famous than it ever was as a sea link between Europe and America. . . ."

The millionaire paused again, to achieve effect.

". . . We are bound, as you know, for Hong Kong. Once there, it will be necessary to carry out some alterations and modifications for that role . . . a role best explained by the new name which will appear on its hull: The University of Freedom. . . ."

There was another pause, this time forced upon him by the sudden burst of noise from the assembled journalists. Lu raised his hand, silencing the room again, then gestured to a bank of seats upon which a group of people had assembled minutes before the commencement of the conference.

"You see behind me," he announced, "professors who have agreed to take Chairs at this university and who have joined me from the Sorbonne, Heidelburg, Oxford, Yale, and Harvard. . . ."

There was a fresh outburst of noise from the journalists and a slight shift in the lighting at the sudden demand for identification.

Lu gestured again.

". . . Some of you may recognise Professor James Northcote, from Harvard, recipient of last year's Nobel Prize in Physics. . . ."

The lights and cameras wavered and a sparse, balding man shuffled awkwardly into a half-standing position and nodded his head.

". . . an indication," took up Lu, bringing the attention back to himself, "of the level of teaching which will be available at my university."

He indicated the man who had opened the conference.

"Under the personal control and organisation of my son, I intend to provide perhaps the best education in the world for students of any nationality. . . ."

He made a deprecatory gesture with his hands.

"There are some of you who may already know a little about me . . ." he said, pausing for the laughter that came from the room and smiling with it. "Those that do will be aware of the steadfast conviction and belief that I have advanced whenever possible . . . a conviction and belief that the free, democratic world is growing increasingly blind to the dangers of communism. . . ."

He sipped from his water glass.

"I believe there is a need for that warning to be repeated, over and over again, until people at last begin to take the proper notice. So upon the University of Freedom, I will provide something more than a superior education. Every undergraduate, no matter what subject he reads, will compulsorily attend daily lectures at which will be fully debated and explained the dangers of the evil, pernicious regime which exists upon the mainland of China. . . ."

Lu rose for the first time, waving his hands to quell the clamour.

". . . a pernicious regime," he repeated, the hiss in his voice more obvious because he had to shout, "which, because of its growing acceptance by the free world, endangers the very existence of democracy. . . ."

Lu remained standing, very aware of his stance and the sound of the cameras recording it, refusing any questions. At last the sound died.

". . . the University of Freedom will be permanently anchored off a small island in the Hong Kong archipelago," he enlarged. "We will be less than five miles from the Chinese mainland . . . a constant and visible reminder to Peking of the truth it tries so hard to suppress. . . ."

Lu sat, nodding to his son. It took fifteen minutes to achieve adherence to a system of questioning that had been established, receiving queries first from the American section and then from the European press. Two hours had been set aside for the conference, but it overran by a further two, so that the liner had to slow and finally turn in a meandering arc upon itself to enable the helicopters to get away just before dark.

The discussions with the assembled academics had been purposely shortened, to guarantee coverage from the journalists travelling in the liner down the east coast to the Panama Canal. The *Pride of America* stopped at Hawaii during its crossing of the Pacific, and Lu chartered another plane to fly in journalists demanding access as the result of the concerted publicity during the voyage.

The arrival in Hong Kong was even more dramatic than the departure from New York. Lu had instructed his tanker and liner fleet to assemble, and the *Pride of America* sailed between the five-mile-long avenue of welcoming, hooting vessels. All the time, it was preceded by two helicopters, between which was supported a massive pennant spelling out its new name, and on the final mile it had to negotiate between fire boats which had introduced dye into their water tanks, to create technicolour fountains of greeting.

It was mid-morning before the Chinese millionaire

and his son reached their house on the far side of the Peak. Immediately they entered the sunken lounge, a servant brought in tea, but it was John Lu who solicitously poured it for his father, standing back and waiting for an indication of approval.

"Very nice," accepted the older man.

John smiled gratefully, the attitude one of constant deference.

"The publicity has been fantastic," he said. He spoke hopefully, anxious his father would agree with the opinion.

Lu nodded. "Like everything, it's a matter of organization."

"Surely you didn't expect this amount of coverage?"

"No," admitted Lu. "Not even I had expected it to go so well."

"Let's hope everything else is so successful," said the younger man.

His father frowned at the doubt. Without an audience, Lu rarely smiled.

"Surely that's been even more carefully organised?"

It was a reminder, not a question.

"Yes," said John hurriedly. "Of course."

"Then we've nothing to worry about."

"I hope not."

"So do I," said Lu. "I hope that very much. . . ."

John's nervousness increased at the tone of his father's voice.

". . . You mustn't forget," continued Lu, "that the whole thing is being done for you."

"I won't forget," said the son. Or be allowed to, he knew.

Jenny Lin Lee had become quiet as the car moved up the winding roads through Hong Kong Heights, actually passing the Lu mansion, and she had realised their destination. By the time Robert Nelson parked outside the Repulse Bay Hotel, she was sitting upright in the passenger seat, staring directly ahead.

"Not here."

"Why not?"

"You know why not."

"Everyone comes here on Sunday."

"Exactly."

"So why shouldn't we?"

"Chinese whores aren't welcome, that's why."

Nelson gripped the wheel, not looking at her.

"You know I don't like that word."

"Because it's the correct one."

"Not any more."

"They don't know that," she said, moving her head towards the open, bougainvillaea-hedged verandah and the restaurant beyond.

"Who gives a damn what they know?"

"I do."

"Why?"

"Because I don't want to shame you in their eyes."

He reached across for her hand, but she kept it rigidly against her knee. She was shaking, he realised.

"I love you, Jenny," he said. "I know what you were and it doesn't offend me. Doesn't even interest me. Any more than what they think interests me. . . ."

She gestured towards the hotel again, an angry movement. He wasn't a very good liar, she decided.

"The rules don't allow it," she said.

"What rules?" he demanded, trying to curb the anger.

"The rules by which the British expatriates live," she said.

He laughed, trying to relax her. She remained stiff in the seat beside him.

"Don't be silly," he pleaded.

"I know them," she insisted. "Had them sweating over me at night and shoving past me in the street with their wives the following morning, contemptuous that I exist."

"Come on," he said, determinedly, getting from the vehicle.

He walked around to the passenger side, opening her door. She stayed, staring ahead.

"Come on," he repeated.

She didn't move.

"Please," he said. He had begun to enunciate clearly, a man intending to show his words and judgment were unaffected by the mid-morning whisky back at the apartment.

She looked up at him, still unable to gauge the effect of drink upon him, but with a professional awareness of its dangers.

"It's a mistake," she warned him.

"No, it's not," he said, reaching out for her.

Reluctantly she got from the car. He took her arm, leading her to the verandah, gazing around defiantly for seats. There were two at the end, with a poor view of the sun-silvered bay and the township of Aberdeen beyond, but he hurried to them, ahead of another couple who emerged from inside the hotel.

The waiter was not slow in approaching them, but Nelson began waving his hands, clapping them together for attention, and when the drinks were finally served, Jenny spilled some of hers in the contagious nervousness and then used too much water trying to remove the stain. It meant there was a large damp patch on her skirt when they finally walked to the buffet line and then to the table he had reserved. Conscious of it, she walked awkwardly. At the table, she ate with her head bent over her plate, rarely looking up when he tried to speak to her.

"They know," she said. "It's like a smell to them."

"No one has even looked at us," he said, trying to reassure her.

"Of course not," she said. "They know. But to them, I do not exist."

The man whose job it had been to prevent Jenny Lin Lee setting up home with Robert Nelson, and who had failed to frighten her, was tied that night beneath the Red Star ferry that crosses the harbour from Kowloon to Hong Kong island in such a way that by straining upwards he could just keep his mouth free of the water, but not far enough for his shouts for help to be heard above the noise of the engine. It took several hours before he became completely exhausted and collapsed back into the water, to drown. And several days before the ropes slackened, releasing the body.

Some time later, already partially decomposed and attacked by fish, it surfaced against the sampans and junks that cling like seaweed to the island side of the harbour.

Knowing it not to be one of them, because sampan people never fall into the water, and with the gypsies' suspicion of the official enquiries it would cause, they poled the corpse along from craft to craft, until it caught in the currents of the open water, near Kai Tak airport, and disappeared out to sea.

The man's disappearance was never questioned. Nor wondered at. Nor reported, either.

CHAPTER TWO

SEVEN THOUSAND MILES and twelve hours apart, there was another lunch that Sunday, as unsuccessful as that of Jenny Lin Lee and Robert Nelson.

Charlie Muffin drove carefully, habitually watchful for any car that remained too long behind. He was unused to the road, too, and was looking for the pub acclaimed three stars in the guide-book. He hoped to Christ it was better than the one the previous week— cottage pie of Saturday's meat scraps, overwarm beer, a bill for £5, and indigestion until Wednesday. At least it had given him something to think about. He sighed, annoyed at the increasingly familiar self-pity. Last time it had almost killed him.

He glanced behind at the thought, checking again, and nearly missed what he was looking for. The Saxon Warrior lay back from the road, an instant antique of sculpted thatch over mock-Tudor beams. Inside he knew there would be mahoganied plastic, fruit machines in every bar and men, wearing blazers and cravats, solving Britain's economic ills while they felt the milled edges of the coins in their pockets to decide if they could buy the next round of drinks.

"Shit," said Charlie fervently. He pulled into the car park and looked at his watch. He hadn't time to find an alternative. Not if he wanted to eat. All he had at the flat was cold beef.

Few people saw Charlie enter, because he didn't want them to and had long ago perfected being unobtrusive. He reached the bar between a group of men to his left re-allocating Britian's oil wealth and a circle to his right undermining communist influence in Africa. The fruit machine was by the toilets. The people around had formed a kitty, in an effort to recover their money before closing time.

The barmaid was a blonde, tightly corseted woman with the bright smile that barmaids share with politicians. Charlie estimated she was about twenty years older than the pub.

"Whiskey," said Charlie, unwilling to risk the beer. There would be no danger, providing he restricted himself to two.

". . . and lunch," he said, when the woman returned with the drink.

"There's mince," she offered doubtfully, looking behind her to the serving hatch.

"No," said Charlie. At least last week they'd disguised it with instant mashed potatoe.

"Bread and cheese?"

"No."

"Beef salad?"

"The guide-book said three stars."

"Trouble in the kitchen."

"Bad day, then?"

"Afraid so."

"Beef salad," said Charlie, resigned. He'd overcooked the meat at home, anyway.

The barmaid retreated to the kitchen hatch and Charlie looked around the bar, sipping his drink. There were pictures of men in flying gear standing alongside Battle of Britain aircraft, a propeller mounted over the bar and, near the counterflap, a man who was obviously the landlord stood frequently touching the tips of a moustache that spread like wings across his face. Mechanic, guessed Charlie. He'd never met a World War II pilot who wore a moustache like that; something to do with the oxygen mask.

Professional as the barmaid, the landlord isolated a new face and detached himself from the African group, moving down the bar. As the man approached, Charlie was aware of the critical examination; the man kept any expression of distaste from his face. Charlie resolved to get his suit pressed. And perhaps buy a new shirt.

"Afternoon," greeted the man.

"Afternoon."

"Sorry about the food. Fire in the kitchen."

"Can't be helped," said Charlie.

"Repaired by next week-end."

"Afraid I won't be here then," said Charlie.

"Didn't think I recognised you. Just passing through?"

"Just passing through," agreed Charlie. As always. Never the same place twice, always polite but distant in any conversation.

"Nice part of the country."

"Very attractive."

"Been here since '48," said the landlord, hand moving automatically to his moustache.

"Straight after the war, then?" said Charlie, joining in the performance. Why not? he thought.

"More or less. You serve?"

"Bit too young," said Charlie. "Berlin airlift was around my time."

"Not the same," dismissed the man.

"So I've heard."

"Had a good war," said the landlord. "Bloody good war."

Charlie avoided any reaction to the cliché. It sounded as obscene now as it had when he had first heard the expression. The bastard who had taken over the department had had a good war. And tried to continue it by setting him up to be killed.

"There were a lot who didn't," said Charlie.

The landlord looked at him curiously, alert for mockery, then relaxed.

"Sorry for them," he said insincerely. "I enjoyed my time."

His glass was empty, Charlie saw. He pushed it across towards the man, to halt the reminiscence.

"Could I have another? Large."

"Certainly."

Charlie knew the man would expect to be bought a drink. But he decided against it, even though it was the first conversation he had had with another person for more than twenty-four hours. He wondered how the man would react to know he was serving whiskey to someone technically a traitor to his country.

The landlord returned with the drink and waited expectantly.

"Thank you," said Charlie.

There was an almost imperceptible shrug as the man took the money and returned Charlie his change.

"What line of business are you in, then?" he asked, lapsing into the pub formula.

"Traveller," said Charlie. It seemed the best description of the aimless life he now led. Even before Edith had been killed they had done little else but move nervously from one place to another.

"Interesting," said the publican, as automatically as he fingered the moustache.

"Sometimes," agreed Charlie.

The woman returned with the salad. The meat had been carefully cut to conceal the dried edges.

"Looks very nice," said Charlie. Insincerity appeared to be infectious. Then again, it was always dangerous to draw attention to himself, even over something as trivial as complaining about a bad meal in a country pub. He manoeuvred himself on to a barstool and the landlord nodded and walked back to his group. Charlie sawed resolutely at the meat, examining his attitude. What right had he to criticise a man for whom the war had been the biggest experience of his life? Or feel contempt for opinionated Sunday lunchtime drinkers? Charlie was always honest with himself, because now there was no one else with whom he could share the trait. And he knew bloody well that he would have gladly handed over the fortune he possessed to change places with any one of them, walking stiff-kneed back to their detached white-painted, executive-style homes to worry about their mortgages and their school fees and their secretaries becoming pregnant. His attitude wasn't really contempt, he recognised. It was envy—envy for people who had wives and mistresses and friends. There was only one person whom Charlie could even think of as a friend. And there had been no contact from Rupert Willoughby for over a year. So perhaps he was even exaggerating that association.

He pushed away the meal half eaten and immediately the barmaid took his plate.

"Like that?" she said.

"Very nice," said Charlie. It was nearly closing time. She would be in a hurry to get away. He hesitated, decided against another drink, and paid his bill. Another £5. And he was regarded as someone who had stolen money!

Back in the car, he sat for a moment, undecided. If he took the B roads and drove slowly, it would be at least seven before he got back to London.

On the balcony of his apartment, high on the island's Mid Level, Robert Nelson stood glass in hand.

"Fantastic," he said, looking down at the *Pride of America*. The liner was an open jewel case of glittering lights. Because it was late, the slur was more noticeable in his voice.

Beside him, Jenny Lin Lee said nothing.

"I've taken eight million of the cover," he announced suddenly.

"What?" she asked, turning to him.

He smiled at her, wanting to boast.

"Lu put the insurance out on the open market. Christ, you should have seen the scramble!"

"But you got £6,000,000 of it?"

"Yes," he said, missing the urgency in her voice. "Beat the bloody lot of them."

He frowned at her lack of reaction.

"I thought you'd be pleased," he complained, petulant in his drunkenness. "No one else got anything like that much. There's already been a cable of congratulation from London . . . signed by Willoughby himself. Even promised a bonus in addition to the commission. . . ."

"If it's important for you, then I'm pleased," she said, turning away from the balcony and the view of the floodlit ship shifting slowly to anchor.

He followed her into the room.

"Sometimes," he said, "I find it completely impossible to understand you."

She stood in the middle of the room, a slim, almost frail figure, the hair, which she constantly used for dramatic effect, cascading to her waist because she knew he liked it worn that way and it was inherent in her to please the man she was with.

She walked to him, smiling for the first time, cupping his head and pulling his face to hers.

"I love you, Robert," she said. "Really love you."

He held her at arm's length, looking at her.

"Why tell me that?" he asked.

"Because I wanted you to know."

The noise of the explosion awoke Nelson and the girl four nights later, as it awoke nearly everyone on the island and the Kowloon waterfront. By the time Nelson got to the balcony, the flames were already spurting from the stem and as he watched there was a noise like a belch and the blaze gushed through the main funnels of the *Pride of America*.

A gradual glow in the stern was the first indication that there was fire there too, then one of the plates burst and huge orange gouts burst out, like a giant exhaust.

"Oh my God," said Nelson softly. He was very sober.

Beside him, the girl remained silent.

Because it was dark, neither could see that the water with which the fire boats were already attacking the blaze was still stained with the welcoming dye. It looked like blood.

CHAPTER THREE

LU HAD WANTED to hold his press conference on the *Pride of America*. But the engine room explosion had blown away plates below the waterline, settling the liner to the top-deck level in the water, and the harbour surveyors forbade the meeting as too dangerous. Instead the Chinese led a small flotilla of boats out to the still-smoking, blackened hull, wheeling around and around in constant focus for the cameras, the customary silk suit concealed beneath protective oilskins and the hard-hat defiantly inscribed "The University of Freedom." John Lu was by his side.

The millionaire had waited four days after the fire for the maximum number of journalists to gather and had to take over the main conference room in the Mandarin Hotel to accommodate them. He entered, still carrying the hat and put it down on the table so that the title would show in any photographs.

He was more impatient than at previous conferences, striding up and down the specially installed platform, calling almost angrily to the microphone for the room to settle.

Finally, disregarding the noise, he began to talk.

"Not a fortnight ago," he said, "I welcomed many of you aboard that destroyed liner out there. . . ."

He swept his hand towards the windows, through which the outline of the ship was visible.

". . . and I announced the purpose to which I was going to put it."

The room was quiet now, the only movement from radio reporters adjusting their sound levels properly to record what Lu was saying.

". . . This morning," he started again, "you have accompanied me into the harbour to see what remains of a once beautiful and proud liner. . . ."

He turned to the table, taking a sheet of paper from a waiting aide.

"This," he declared, "is the surveyor's preliminary report. Copies will be made individually available as you leave this room. But I can sum it up for you in just two words—'totally destroyed.'"

He turned again, throwing the paper onto the table and taking another held out in readiness for him, this time by John Lu.

"This is another report . . . that of investigators who have for the past four days examined the ship to discover the cause of the fire . . ." continued Lu. "This will also be made available. But again I will summarise it . . ."

He indicated behind him, to where two men in uniform sat, files on their knees.

". . . and I have asked the men who prepared the report to attend with me today should there later at this conference be any questions you might like to put to them. Their findings are quite simple. The *Pride of America* has been totally destroyed as the result of carefully planned, carefully instigated acts of arson. . . ."

He raised his hand, ahead of the reaction to the announcement.

". . . Arson," he went on. "Devised so that it guaranteed the *Pride of America* would never be able to be put to the use that I intended. . . ."

He referred to the report in his hand.

". . . 'Large quantity of inflammable material spread throughout cabins in the forward section,' " he quoted. " 'Sprinkler system disconnected and inoperative and fire doors jammed to prevent closing . . . debris of two explosive devices in the engine room, together with more inflammable material, ensuring immediate and possibly uncontrollable fire . . . kerosene introduced into the sprinkler system at the rear of the vessel so that the fire would be actually fed by those attempting to extinguish it. . . .' "

He looked up for what he was saying to be assimilated.

". . . Provable, incontrovertible facts," he said. "As provable and as incontrovertible as this. . . ."

Again the aide was waiting, handing to Lu a length of twisted, apparently partially melted metal about a foot long. The millionaire held it before him, turning to the photographers' shouted requests.

". . . There is some lettering upon the side," he said, pointing to it with his finger and once more holding it for the benefit of the cameramen. "A translation will be made available, together with all the other documents to which I've referred today. But again I will summarise it for you. This is part of the outer casing of an incendiary device. It was found, together with other evidence still in possession of the Hong Kong police, in the engine room. The lettering positively identifies it as manufactured in the People's Republic of China. . . ."

Lu returned the casing to the table behind him, happy now for the noise to build up.

"Arson," he shouted above the clamour. "Arson committed by a country frightened of having the free world constantly reminded of the evils of its doctrine. . . ."

He snatched again for the incendiary casing.

". . . Their former leader, Mao Tse-tung, once preached that power comes from the barrel of a gun. This is the proof of that doctrine. . . ."

He slumped back against the table, reaching out for

the instantly available glass of water, and throughout the room more aides began moving with microphones so that questions would be heard by everyone.

"Do you feel fully justified in making the accusations that you have today?" was the first, from an unseen woman at the back.

Lu led the mocking laughter that broke out.

"I've rarely felt so justified of anything in my life," he said. "Is it possible for a country to sue someone for defamation of character? If it is, then I shall be happy to accept any writ from the People's Republic of China."

"Will you attempt to buy another vessel to create another University of Freedom?" asked the New York *Times* correspondent.

"And have it burned out within days! That blackened hulk out there can speak as eloquently as any political lecturer of the dangers I wanted to publicise."

"What about the professors whom you had already engaged?" demanded the same questioner.

"They were employed upon a year's contract. In every case, that contract has been honoured in full and first-class air fares made available to return them to whichever country they chose."

"How much has all this cost?"

"I have never made any secret of the fact that I purchased the *Pride of America* for $20,000,000."

"Does that mean you've lost that amount of money?" queried an Englishman representing the Far East Economic Review.

"Of course not. International Maritime regulations insist that it should be fully insured."

"So the $20,000,000 is recoverable?"

"Certainly I shall be eventually reimbursed for the purchase of the vessel. But that, gentlemen, isn't important. What is important is for the world to recognise the flagrant reaction of a country terrified of the truth . . . and the lengths to which it is prepared to go to prevent that truth. . . ."

"Who were the insurers?" asked the Englishman.

"The cover was spread through several consortium of Lloyds, of London."

"Is the claim already submitted?"

"Probably," said Lu dismissively. "I've left the matter in the hands of my lawyers."

Two days after Lu's publicised conference, an announcement was made in the name of Chief Superintendant Sydney Johnson, of the Hong Kong police. As a result of intensive enquiries since the arson aboard the *Pride of America,* it said, Hong Kong detectives had arrested two Chinese who had been employed aboard the vessel for its modification refit. Investigation had shown them to be mainland Chinese who had illegally crossed the border into Hong Kong only six months previously. Their families still resided in Shanghai.

On this occasion, Lu did not summon a conference. Instead he issued a brief statement. Without wishing to prejudice any court hearing, it said, the police announcement was regarded as proof of every claim made by Mr. L. W. Lu, who looked forward with interest to a full judicial examination of the arrested men.

Both men were hesitant, each unsure of the other.

"I wasn't sure if you'd come," said Rupert Willoughby.

Charlie Muffin walked further into the underwriter's office, taking the outstretched hand.

"Never thought I'd get beyond the secretary," said Charlie, indicating the outer office.

"She's a little over-protective at times," apologised Willoughby. It was easy to understand his secretary's reluctance. Charlie still wore the concertinaed suit he remembered from their last encounter, like a helper behind the second-hand clothes stall at a Salvation Army hostel. The thatch of strawish hair was still disordered about his face, and the Hush Puppies were as scuffed and down-at-heel as always.

"Your call surprised me," said Charlie. Willoughby was the only person who possessed his telephone number. Or the knowledge of what he had once been. And done.

"I had decided you'd never call," he added.

"I almost didn't," admitted Willoughby.

"So you're in trouble?"

"Big trouble," agreed Willoughby. "I don't see any way of getting out."

"Which makes me the last resort?"

"Yes," said the underwriter, "I suppose it does."

CHAPTER FOUR

RUPERT WILLOUGHBY was a tall, ungainly man, constantly self-conscious of his height. He took great care with his tailoring, trying to minimise his stature, but almost always hunched, trying to reduce it further. He crouched now, blond hair flopping over his forehead as he bent over his desk, occasionally referring to a file as he outlined the details of the *Pride of America* cover, every so often jerking up to the other man, as if in expectation of some reaction.

Beyond the desk, Charlie sat with his legs splayed before him, head sunk upon his chest. By twisting his left foot very slightly, Charlie could see that the repair hadn't worked and that the sole of his left shoe was parting from the uppers. Which was a bloody nuisance. It meant a new pair, and those he was wearing were at last properly moulded to his feet. It always seemed to happen like that, just when he got comfortable. Looked like rain, too.

". . . and so," concluded Willoughby, "our consortium appears liable for the entire £6,000,000."

"Yes," said Charlie. "It appears you are."

How much the man resembled his father, thought Charlie, nostalgically. Practically an identical style of setting out a problem, an orderly collection of facts from which any opinion or assessment was kept rigidly apart so that no preconceptions could be formed. Sir Archibald Willoughby, who had headed the department during almost all of Charlie's operational career and whom Charlie realised without embarrassment he had come to regard as a father-figure, had obviously groomed his real son very carefully.

"It's a lot of money to lose," said the underwriter.

The figure was too large to consider seriously, decided Charlie. He looked sideways. How much space in the room would £6,000,000 occupy, he wondered, idly. The whole bookcase and the sidetable, certainly. Probably overflow on to the couch as well.

"And you want to avoid paying out?"

Willoughby stared across the desk. His hand was twitching, Charlie saw.

"It might be difficult," said the underwriter hurriedly. The admission embarrassed him and he actually blushed.

"You haven't got your share!" demanded Charlie.

"No."

"Christ."

"It's only temporary," said Willoughby defensively. "We've had a very bad two years . . . whole series of setbacks."

"But why take the risk, in the first place?"

"I *had* to," insisted Willoughby. "A firm can be wiped out in a creditors' rush by no more than a City rumour that it's in financial difficulties. Besides which, there seemed *no* risk."

"You're a bloody fool," said Charlie.

"That knowledge doesn't help, either," said Willoughby.

"Your father left a fortune," remembered Charlie.

"Already gone."

"Loans then."

"There's hardly a bank where I don't have an overdraft. And where I haven't gone over the limit."

"So?"

"So unless there's a near miracle, there's nothing that can stop me being drummed out of the Exchange."

"Nobody knows?"

"Nobody. Yet. But it won't take long. This sort of news never does."

"What's the legal opinion of Lu's claim?"

"We are completely liable," said Willoughby.

"No room for manoeuvre?"

Willoughby shook his head. "We might have had a chance had we included a political sabotage clause . . . the sort of thing that's been introduced into aircraft cover since hijacking started."

"Why didn't you?"

"Because it's not normal, in case of ship cover . . . and I was in too much of a hurry to sign the policy."

"Why?"

"Nelson managed to negotiate a 12 per cent premium . . . for Lloyds; that's very high. I needed the liquidity."

"Who's Nelson?"

"Our Hong Kong agent."

"Good?"

"He got more of the cover than anyone else when it was put upon the Hong Kong market."

"Why?"

"Why what?"

"Why more than anybody else . . . at such a good premium?"

"Because he's better, I suppose. Or because he tried harder."

"What's he like?"

"Unusual chap," remembered the underwriter. "I've only met him three times. Colonial, through and through. Born in India, father a governor for a minor state there before independence. Only time spent in England was at school—Eton and then Cambridge. He's so out of place here that two years ago he cut short the paid home leave that we allow our overseas men. Made some excuse about the climate."

"Reliable?"

"Absolutely."

"What does he say?"

Willoughby paused at the staccato questioning.

"It's so straightforward that he doesn't even see the need for an investigation," he said.

"But you do?"

Willoughby came forward over the desk.

"I've got to try," he said. "I've got to try anything."

The soul-baring would be difficult for the man, Charlie knew. He'd hate admitting to being anything less than his father had been.

"How long before you've got to pay?" asked Charlie.

Willoughby made a movement of uncertainty.

"Lu's lawyers have already filed an intention to claim. We could probably delay until the two men who have been arrested are found guilty, but even to attempt that might create a dispute. I gather they've made a full admission."

"So you haven't much time?"

"I haven't much of anything," said Willoughby. "Time least of all."

"The last resort," repeated Charlie. There was no point in buggering about. And Willoughby appeared to appreciate honesty, anyway.

"Yes," agreed the underwriter.

"Would you have avoided contacting me, if you could?" demanded Charlie.

Willoughby paused. Then he admitted: "Yes. If I had had a choice, I wouldn't have made the call."

Most people would have lied, recognised Charlie, unoffended. The man was trying to retain his integrity, anxious though he was.

"Well?" said Willoughby. He couldn't keep the plea out of his voice.

So much of his life had been spent getting hold of the shitty end of the stick that nobody else wanted to touch, reflected Charlie. How much he wished the approach had come through friendship rather than desperation. He had very much wanted the sort of association he had known with the man's father.

"Why should I?" he said.

". . . *Why make people crawl, Charlie. . . . Why bully . . . ?*"

The part of him that had always embarrassed Edith most, he remembered. The part his wife didn't like and was always trying to correct.

Willoughby winced, imagining a rejection.

"No reason," he accepted. "The sort of things you once did . . ."

He paused, recalling what Charlie had done.

". . . It was silly of me," he said. "I should have realised you couldn't do it . . . that it would be too dangerous for you because of what happened."

"You expect me to . . . because of my relationship with your father?"

"I *hoped* you'd try to help."

"As the last resort."

"Please," said Willoughby.

Charlie stopped, suddenly angry with himself. He shouldn't do it, certainly not to a man whose father had befriended him to the degree that Sir Archibald had.

"*. . . inverted snobbery. . . .*"

Another of Edith's accusations. Almost correct, too. Sir Archibald had recognised it properly. Warned him about it, even.

"*. . . inferiority complex, Charlie . . . not the confidence everyone imagines. Why, Charlie . . . ?*"

And Charlie couldn't answer because he hadn't known himself. Not then. Not until it was too late.

"I'm sorry," he said to the other man.

"You've a right to be offended," accepted Willoughby. "It was madness of me to think of you, after all you've been through."

"Not really," said Charlie. "You didn't put up barriers when I asked you for help once."

It had been after Charlie had allowed the stupid mistake and made the pilgrimage to Sir Archibald's grave. British intelligence had picked him up there and started the pursuit. What logic said it had been all right for them to set him up to be killed in East Berlin, then label him a renegade, to be hunted and assassinated because he had fought back and exposed them for their stupidity? Only Willoughby had understood because the same men had caused his father's suicide. So only Willoughby had helped. Not true, he corrected. Edith had helped, like she always had done. And now Edith was dead.

Believing he had been rejected, Willoughby said: "I'd appreciate your not mentioning this to anyone."

"I haven't said I wouldn't help," said Charlie.

Willoughby blinked, his eagerness almost childishly obvious in his face.

"You could get to Hong Kong?" he said hurriedly. "I mean, there wouldn't be any difficulty with . . . about your identity . . . ?"

Charlie smiled at the other man's renewed embarrassment.

"The passport is genuine enough," he said. "It was the documents that obtained it that were phoney."

Work again, thought Charlie. Different from what he'd been used to, but still work. It would be good to get back. And to end those aimless Sunday drives.

"I'd need the full authority of your company," said Charlie. "I'd never get official help without it."

"Of course," accepted Willoughby. "And I'll let Nelson know you're coming. . . . Ask him to give you every assistance."

Charlie stood.

". . . And thank you," said Willoughby.

"There's no guarantee that I'll find anything to help you," warned Charlie. "It seems as straightforward as Nelson has said."

"But you might," said the underwriter.

The man was more desperate than he had imagined, decided Charlie as he emerged into the secretary's office. The summer rain suddenly burst against the window and he remembered the split sole.

"Where's the nearest shoe shop?" he said.

The girl looked up to Charlie in hostile bewilderment.

"A what?"

"Shoe shop," repeated Charlie. Supporting himself against her desk, he raised his foot, so she could see the gap.

"Need a new pair," he said unnecessarily.

The girl pressed back against her chair, face frozen in contempt.

"I'm sure I really have no idea," she said.

Charlie lowered his foot but remained leaning on her desk.

"Never make a Girl Guide," he said.

"And you'll never make a comedian."

It would have to stop, decided Charlie, as he left the building. Now he was trying to score off simple secretaries, just because they had posh accents. And losing.

At first Robert Nelson had tolerated Jenny's insistence, regarding it more as something like a secret intimacy between them. But as the months had passed and she had maintained the demand, he had come to regard it as a humiliation to them both.

She sat, waiting on the opposite side of the table. Beside her lay the wallet, various pouches unzipped and ready.

"Housekeeping," he said, counting out the money.

Sipping from his drink, he watched her put it carefully into the top section of her wallet. He'd managed at last to persuade her there was no need for written details of the household accounts, so perhaps the other thing wouldn't be difficult.

"Dress allowance," he said.

She nodded, smiling.

He took another drink, both hands clasped around his glass.

She sat, waiting.

"Please, Robert," she said, frowning.

"Why, for Christ's sake!"

His annoyance broke through so that he spoke louder than he had intended.

"Please," she said again.

He put the glass aside, determined against another outburst, spacing his words in an effort to convince her.

"Apart form a stupid piece of paper, you are my wife," he said gently. "I love you and want you to stay with me. Always."

"I know," she said.

"Then why?"

"Because it's always been . . . since I was young . . ."

"It's . . . it's obscene," he protested, realising he had failed again.

"Please," she said persistently.

Angrily he pushed into his pocket, bringing out more notes and thrusting them onto the table.

"I-love-you money," he itemised.

"Thank you," she said, putting the money into a waiting pouch.

How long would it take, wondered Nelson, for her to forget what she had once been?

CHAPTER FIVE

IT WAS THE TIE that registered with Charlie, long before Robert Nelson got near enough for a formal greeting. So long ago, thought Charlie. Yet so easily recalled. Blue stripes upon blue, at an angle.

The two men who had set him up to be killed on the East Berlin border had been to Eton. And like Robert Nelson had always worn their ties, no matter the colour of their suits. An identification symbol, decided Charlie, like road signs—something to be recognised by everyone.

They'd mocked his grammar-school accent. And the way he'd dressed. So they'd underestimated him, dismissing him as an anachronism—a perfect sacrifice. And been so disastrously wrong. Only one had survived, remembered Charlie. And he'd ensured the man had been disgraced. Twice. But he would still be wearing the tie, wherever he was, Charlie knew.

"I've kept you waiting," apologised Nelson, reaching him at last through the airport crowd.

"I've only just cleared customs," assured Charlie,

31

immediately conscious of the swirl of harassed agitation in which the insurance broker moved.

A strangely pale, almost flakey-skinned man, Robert Nelson was sweating, despite the thin suit and the partial air conditioning, so that the wisped, receding hair was smeared over his forehead, accentuating the pallor.

Even before their handshake had ended, he was gesturing impatiently to porters whom Charlie had already engaged, sighing with frustration at people who had innocently intruded themselves between the luggage, and twice muttering "Sorry, so very sorry" to Charlie, in regret for some imagined hindrance.

The air conditioning was better within the confined space of the waiting car and Nelson mopped his face and hands with an already damp handkerchief, smiling across the vehicle. It was an apprehensive expression, decided Charlie. Why? he wondered.

"I knew there would be an investigation," announced Nelson, as if confirming an earlier discussion. "Just knew it."

"Routine, surely?" said Charlie. He looked at his watch. Whiskey-breathed at ten in the morning?

"But you're not one of the normal investigators. Director level, Willoughby said."

"No," said Charlie. "Not a normal investigator."

Despite his assurances to Willoughby, there was still a risk of someone discovering just how different, he knew. His hand still had the slight shake that had started when he had approached the passport and immigration desks at the airport.

Nelson appeared to be expecting more but, when Charlie didn't continue, pointed through the window.

"You can just see the *Pride of America*," he said.

Charlie gazed out into the bay, getting a brief view of the hull before the car dipped into the tunnel that would take them beneath the harbour to Hong Kong island.

"Looks a very dead ship," said Charlie.

"It is."

"Any scrap value?"

"Less than a million, I would estimate. I believe the Japanese are already interested."

"Quite a difference from $20,000,000."

"Yes," agreed Nelson, as if appreciating some hidden point. "Quite a difference."

The vehicle emerged from the tunnel and turned along the Connaught Road towards the Mandarin Hotel. To the right, towards Kowloon, the seemingly disordered slick of sampans and junks locked one to the other and stretched far out into the bay from the harbour edge. So tight was the jam that it was impossible to identify occupant with craft, and the impression was of constant, heaving movement, like a floating anthill.

"They're called the floating people," said Nelson. "It's said that some are born, live, and die without ever coming ashore."

Charlie turned to his left, looking inland. A mile away first the Middle Level, then the Heights jutted upwards to the Peak, the apartment blocks and villas glued against the rock edges.

"Easy to judge the wealth here," said Nelson, nodding in the direction in which Charlie was looking. "The higher you live, the richer you are."

"What about Lu?"

"One of the richest taipans in the entire colony," said Nelson. "He's got a villa on the other side of the Peak, at Shousan Hill. Like a fortress."

"Why a fortress?"

"Ensure his privacy."

"I thought Lu enjoyed exposure and publicity."

"Exactly," said Nelson. "It makes him an obvious target for every crank and crook in Asia."

Nelson flustered around the arrival at the hotel, urging bellboys over the bags and actually cupping Charlie's elbow to guide him into the hotel.

The broker hovered beside him while he registered, instantly chiding the porters when they turned from the reception desk, and Charlie sighed. Nelson's attitude could very easily become a pain in the ass, he thought.

It was the briefest of impressions as they waited for

the elevator, but Charlie had been trained to react to such feelings and he twisted abruptly, examining the foyer.

"What is it?" demanded Nelson, conscious of the sudden movement.

"Nothing," said Charlie.

He's always had an instinct about surveillance, he remembered. But he *had* to be wrong. How could he be so quickly under observation? And from whom? There was no reason. He was jet-lagged and irritated by Nelson's constant attention, that was it.

The lift arrived and Charlie started to enter, pausing at the entrance. He'd survived by responding to impressions as fleeting as this. And while he'd changed vocations, the need for survival remained. More so. Now that he'd come out of hiding.

"Sure there's nothing wrong?" said Nelson.

Charlie stared back into the bustling foyer.

"Quite sure," he said absently.

Nelson had reserved him a suite and Charlie examined it appreciatively.

"Never get this on Civil Service Grade IV allowance," he said softly. Self-conversation was a habit he never bothered to curb. It usually became more pronounced when he was worried.

"What?" asked Nelson.

"Thinking aloud," said Charlie. Obviously Robert Nelson had no idea of his company's financial difficulties.

"I got a bar installed," pointed out Nelson hopefully.

"Help yourself," invited Charlie.

"You?"

"Too tired after the flight," said Charlie, watching the other man reach for the whisky.

Islay malt, he saw. Sir Archibald had been drinking that, when he'd gone to his retirement home in Sussex the day before setting off to entrap the bastards who had taken over the department and reduced it to an apology of what it had once been.

There'd been bottles of it in a sitting room cupboard. The poor old sod had fallen into a drunken sleep and not been aware when he had left. According to the inquest report, Sir Archibald had even swilled the barbiturates down with it.

"I specified a room with a view of the harbour. And Kowloon," said Nelson, by the window.

"Thank you," said Charlie. "The ship, too."

"Yes," agreed Nelson. "Everywhere I look I'm reminded of that damned ship."

Charlie turned to the man, curious at the bitterness.

"And beyond the New Territories is China," continued Nelson, with his back to the room.

"I know."

"You've been to Hong Kong before?"

"No," said Charlie quickly, alert to questions about his past.

"Incidentally," said Nelson, apparently unaware of Charlie's apprehensive reaction, "Australia are ninety-six for two."

The broker had turned back into the suite and Charlie stared at him in astonishment.

"What?" he said.

"The Test," said the broker, disconcerted by Charlie's lack of response. "We get the reports on the BBC World service."

"Oh," said Charlie. And no doubt discussed the finer points in the clubs and the cocktail parties and couldn't have located Lords or the Oval with a street map.

"You're not interested in cricket?"

"Not really," admitted Charlie. What was it that the man was finding so much difficulty in saying?

Nelson looked at his glass, appearing surprised that it was empty.

"Go ahead," gestured Charlie.

Nelson remained at the portable bar, looking across the room.

"I'm to be dismissed, aren't I?" he demanded suddenly.

Charlie frowned at him.

"What . . . ?"

"That's why you've come . . . someone who's not a

normal investigator . . . a director. You've come to fire me because there was no qualifying clause in the policy."

The fear tumbled from the man; the words blurred together in his anxiety.

"Of course you're not," said Charlie.

He reached down, easing off his shoes.

"You must excuse me," he said. "They're new. Pinch like hell."

Nelson gazed at the other man, controlling the look that had begun to settle on his face. Old Etonians didn't take their shoes off in public, decided Charlie. Careful, he thought. That was an antagonism of another time.

"Yours was not the final decision on the policy," he reminded, straightening. "You drew it up, certainly. And admittedly it's an expensive oversight that there was no political-sabotage clause. But London gave the final approval. You're not being held responsible."

"I find that difficult to believe. . . . I negotiated it, after all."

"Very successfully, according to Willoughby."

Nelson moved away from the bar, his suspicion of the remark obvious.

"What do you mean?"

"Wasn't 12 per cent high?"

"Comparatively so."

"That's exactly what I want to do, compare. What were the other premiums?"

"I don't know," said Nelson uncomfortably. "It was sealed bids. Lu kept me waiting until the very last moment . . . wanted more time . . . all done in a terrible rush, really."

So convinced was he of dismissal that despite Charlie's attempted reassurance, Nelson could still not avoid offering a defence.

"And you haven't enquired about the other premiums?"

Nelson shook his head, embarrassed at the oversight.

"Another cause for complaint," he said, resigned.

"I've told you. No one's blaming you," repeated Charlie. He would telephone Willoughby to get a confirmatory letter.

"It'll be a disaster for the firm, won't it?" demanded Nelson.

More than you know, thought Charlie.

"If they have to pay," he said.

The qualification penetrated the other man's nervousness and he came closer to where Charlie was sitting.

"*If?*"

"I've flown seven thousand miles to decide if we should," reminded Charlie.

"But we've no grounds for resisting settlement," said Nelson.

"Not yet," agreed Charlie.

"Do you think I haven't examined every single thing that's happened since the damned explosion?" said Nelson, as if his ability were being questioned afresh. "There's nothing wrong with Lu's claim . . . not a bloody thing."

"But you still don't know what the other premiums were."

"I'm *sorry*," said Nelson, exasperation breaking through.

"Can you find out?"

"The other companies might not want to disclose it."

"Isn't there an old boys' network?" demanded Charlie. Surely there were more blue-patterned ties in Hong Kong?

Nelson hesitated before replying.

"I'll try," he promised. "But I don't see what it would prove."

"Might not prove anything," admitted Charlie. "Then again, it might be interesting. I think we should look a little deeper, that's all. Get under the surface."

Nelson went back to the window, looking now not out over the harbour but down into the streets far below.

"This might be an English colony," he said reflectively. "But it's China down there, in almost everything but name. . . ."

He turned back to Charlie.

". . . Westerners aren't allowed beneath any surface here. We're tolerated, that's all."

"Nowhere can be as closed as that," protested Charlie.

"Hong Kong is," insisted Nelson. "Believe me. If there were anything wrong with the fire, we wouldn't find it from the Chinese community."

"But there isn't anything wrong, as far as you're concerned?"

Nelson shook his head.

"I wish there were," he said. "God knows I've tried hard enough to find it. But the evidence is overwhelming."

"The police are being co-operative?"

"They've no reason not to be, with a case like they've got."

He indicated a briefcase.

"I've brought the file for you."

Charlie smiled his thanks.

"So you think we'll have to pay out?"

Nelson's belief that the fire was uncontestable would have been another reason for imagining that a directorial visit was to announce his dismissal, realised Charlie.

"I *know* we'll have to pay," confirmed the broker. "Lucky Lu never suffers misfortune that costs him money."

"Lucky?"

"His wealth started with some deals that turned out spectacularly successful on the Hong Kong stock exchange. It's been Lucky Lu for as long as I can remember."

"Sounds like a poof's favourite lavatory," reflected Charlie, massaging his feet. It would take weeks to break those damned shoes in, he knew. It had been wise to postpone having the supports put in.

"You're very different from what I expected," said

Nelson suddenly. "I think other people are going to be surprised, too."

"Other people?"

"I assumed you'd want to see the police chief. Name's Johnson. I mentioned your coming. And I told Lu's people as well. Willoughby asked me to give you all the help I could."

"Thanks," said Charlie. He'd have preferred announcing his own presence.

"You're annoyed," said Nelson, detecting the reservation in Charlie's voice and growing immediately apprehensive.

"No," lied Charlie. Poor bugger seemed worried at his own shadow; but then, so were they all for different reasons.

"Is there anything else I can do?"

Charlie shook his head.

"I suppose I'd better study the file. And get some sleep."

The broker stayed for another drink before leaving Charlie, promising to collect him the following morning so they could attend the remand hearing of the two Chinese accused of arson.

Alone, Charlie closed all the curtains against the view and the sunlight, put a "Do Not Disturb" notice outside the room, and decided the file could wait.

He slept for about five hours and then awoke, knowing it was still not midnight Hong Kong time and that he had long hours of sleeplessness ahead of him.

Edith would have enjoyed the luxury of the apartment, he decided, feeling his eyes cloud in the darkness. And tried so hard to conceal her concern at the cost. Poor Edith. Always so aware of the money. And of his resentment at her inheritance sufficient to support them both.

And it had been resentment, he recognised. The perpetual feeling. Idiotic, childlike resentment. He could even recall the words he'd shouted at her, careless of the hurt, when she had suggested he simply retire from the service which had decided he was expendable and live on her wealth.

"*. . . and don't patronise me with your money . . . like you've always patronised me with your breeding. . . .*"

That was why he had inveigled America and the $500,000 defection fund, he knew. To ensure there would never be any dependence upon her. Why in God's name hadn't he realised how truly dependent he had been, instead of turning them both into exiles, terrified of every footstep?

"I'm sorry, darling," he said. "So very sorry."

He didn't want to spend more than a month in Hong Kong, he decided. The grave would start to become too overgrown if he were any longer.

Sighing, he snapped on the light and pulled the file towards him. He'd be bloody tired in the morning, he knew.

There had been two supplementary reports to the original account from the CIA's Asian station in Hong Kong and then a separate analysis prepared by specialists at the Langley headquarters in Virginia.

"Well?" demanded the Director.

"Certainly looks like Peking," judged the Deputy.

"Odd though."

"Facts are there."

"We've got to be sure."

"Of course."

"Why don't we send in someone with no preconceptions, to work independent of the station?"

"They won't like it."

"I'm more interested in being able to advise the President and the Secretary of State that China is growing careless of détente than I am with the feelings of some station personnel," said the Director sharply.

"Who?" asked the Deputy.

"Someone who's been . . . anxious to prove himself. . . ."

Harvey Jones heard the telephone ringing as he pedalled up Q-Street at the end of his daily five-mile ride. He sprinted the last few yards, ran up the steps, and fumbled the key into the lock to snatch it off the rest as the ringing was about to stop.

"There you are," said the Deputy Director, annoyed at being kept waiting. "Thought for a moment that you were going to miss the chance of a lifetime."

CHAPTER SIX

THE AUTHORITIES had not anticipated the demand for admission to the remand hearing and had only assigned one of the smaller courts, with limited seating, so that entry had to be controlled by permit.

"I managed to get two," reported Nelson in the car taking them to the administrative building. "It wasn't easy, though. The press are screaming for all the seats."

"We were lucky then," said Charlie. Like the tie, the broker retained the harassed anxiety of the previous day. And a dampness was already softening his shirt and suit into creases. The man was still unconvinced his job was safe.

The discovery of the other premiums, Charlie knew.

"You're quite sure that the rest were only 10 per cent?"

Nelson saw the reiteration as criticism. He was annoyed, too, that such an obvious enquiry hadn't occurred to him in advance of the man's arrival from London.

"Yes," he said tightly. "Those I could find out about, anyway."

"Still convinced that there's nothing strange about the fire?" said Charlie.

"It's odd," conceded Nelson.

"Odd enough to look further?"

"I've told you how difficult that will be."

"There's the police," said Charlie. And the personal danger in approaching them. Overcautious, he told himself. How could there by any danger here in Hong Kong? It was, he recognised, an apprehension of authority. Any authority. It would always be with him. Like so many other fears.

The car began to slow at the approach to the administrative buildings.

"It shouldn't last long," said Nelson.

"Remand hearings usually don't."

"You've been to a lot?"

Charlie tensed, then relaxed. There was no danger in the admission.

"Quite a few," he said.

But not the sort Nelson imagined. Always before, it had involved sneaking through side doors and adjoining buildings, to avoid the surveillance and cameras of those uncaptured for Official Secret trials of those who had been caught and who nearly always reminded Charlie of the grey, anonymous people at rush-hour bus queues. Which was why, he supposed, they had made such good spies. Until he had exposed them.

"Have you anything planned for tonight?" asked Nelson abruptly.

Charlie turned to him in the car, curiously.

"There's a very good Peking-style restaurant in the Gloucester Road, and Jenny and I wondered if you'd like to be our guest."

Chinatown with English county street names, reflected Charlie. Why, he wondered, had Nelson blurted the invitation with even more urgency than was customary?

"Jenny?" he queried.

". . . My . . . she's . . . someone I live with . . ."

said Nelson awkwardly. As if the qualification were necessary, he added, "Jenny Lin Lee."

"I'd like very much to eat with you," accepted Charlie. Again the need for hurried words, he recognised. There was embarrassment mixed with Nelson's permanent agitation.

Because of the crush around the building, they left the car some distance away, and as soon as they began walking Charlie felt the prickle of unseen attention. He started around quickly, as he had in the hotel foyer, but again could detect nothing.

Apprehension of the cameras, he decided, as they got to the steps. Expertly Charlie manoeuvred himself behind Nelson, watching for a casually pointed lens which might record him in the background of a picture and lead to an accidental identification from someone with a long memory.

It was cooler inside the building, although Nelson did not appear to benefit.

"There's the police chief," said Nelson, pointing across the entrance hall to a tall, heavily built man.

"Superintendent Johnson," called the broker.

The man turned, a very mannered, slow movement. Like Willoughby, the policeman had an affectation involving his height. But unlike the underwriter, Johnson accentuated his size, leaning slightly back and gazing down with his chin against his chest, calculated always to make the person he was addressing feel inferior.

"The senior colleague from London about whom I told you," introduced Nelson.

Johnson examined Charlie.

"*Senior* colleague?" he queried pointedly. He was immaculate, uniform uncreased, buttons gleaming and the collar so heavily starched it was already scoring a red line around his neck."

"Yes," confirmed Nelson, appearing unaware of the condescension.

Hesitantly, Johnson offered his hand.

Charlie smiled, remembering Nelson's remark of the previous evening about the surprise of people he would

encounter. Underestimated again, he thought, contentedly.

"Investigating the fire," added Nelson thoughtlessly.

Johnson's reaction was immediate.

"It has already been investigated," he said stiffly.
"And satisfactorily concluded."

"Of course," said Charlie smoothly. "These things
are routine."

Johnson continued staring at him. Unconsciously the
man was wiping his hand against the side of his
trousers.

"Ever been in the Force?" invited Johnson.

Another recognition symbol, decided Charlie. Like a
tie.

"No," he admitted. It meant a closed door, he knew.

"Scotland Yard," announced Johnson, as if produc-
ing a reference. "Fifteen years. Never an unsolved
case."

"Just like this one?"

Johnson put his head to one side, trying to detect
the sarcasm.

"Yes," he said positively. "Just like this one."

"I rather wondered if it might be possible for you
and me to meet . . . at your convenience, obviously,"
said Charlie.

"I've already made everything I considered applica-
ble available to Mr. Nelson," said the superintendent.

"I know," said Charlie. "I've read your reports.
You've really been most helpful. There are just one or
two things that seem unusual. . . ."

"I've a busy diary. . . ."

". . . Of course," flattered Charlie. Pompous prick,
he thought.

". . . lot of commitments."

"It wouldn't take more than fifteen minutes," persisted Charlie. "There's a huge sum of money involved,
after all."

"Talk to my secretary," capitulated Johnson. "We
will see what we can do tomorrow."

"You're very kind," said Charlie. Between what

would he be fitted? he wondered. Golf? Or the yacht club lunch?

An usher announced that the court was about to convene, interrupting them. There was a slow shuffle through the entrance, bottlenecked by two of Johnson's officers scrutinising the entry tickets. Nelson and Charlie were allocated to the well of the tiny court, just to the left and below the dock. Charlie twisted as the men were arraigned, looking up at them. Why was it that criminals never had the stature expected of their crimes? The two accused Chinese entered the dock cowed and frightened, heads twitching like animals suspecting a trap about to close behind them. One wore just trousers and vest, and the second had a jacket, grimed and shapeless from constant use, over a collarless shirt. The man's trousers were supported by cord. Charlie recognised the habitual opium habit from the yellowed, jaundiced look of their eyes. Their bodies vibrated with the denial imposed since their arrest.

Charlie turned away, stopping at the sight of Johnson rigidly upright and towering above the other policemen at the far side of the dock. The sort of man, judged Charlie, who would stand up before he farted in the bath. Probably at attention. Johnson looked directly at him, his face blank.

At the demand from the usher, the court stood for the entry of the magistrate. Immediately he was seated, the clerk announced that the accusation would be read first in English, then translated into Cantonese for the benefit of the accused.

"The charge against you," began the official, looking first to the dock and then back to the charge sheet, ". . . is that on June 10 you did jointly commit an offence of arson, namely that you did secrete aboard a liner known as the *Pride of America* incendiary devices and that further you did, separately and together, ignite at various situations aboard the said liner quantities of inflammable material. Further, it is alleged that you interfered with the fire-precaution systems upon the said liner in such a way that additional quantities of inflammable material were introduced into the flames. . . ."

He stopped, handing the sheet to the Chinese interpreter.

The man began the accusation, but was almost immediately stopped by a noise which Charlie later realised must have been the sound of the first man falling. He turned at the scuffling movement, in time to see the warders move forward to try to prevent the second Chinese, in the crumpled jacket, from collapsing beneath the dock rail.

There was a moment of complete, shocked silence broken only by the unseen sound from the dock of strained, almost screaming attempts to breathe, and then it was overwhelmed by the babble that erupted as reporters tried to get nearer the dock, to look in.

Then there was another commotion, as Superintendent Johnson started ordering his policemen at a bellow, trying to restore order.

A warder emerged from below the rail, and there was a second momentary lull in the noise.

"Dead," announced the man. "They're both dead."

He spoke apologetically, as if he might in some way be blamed for it.

Superintendent Johnson succeeded in interposing constables between the dock and people trying to stare in, and then more officers arrived to clear the court.

It was not until they were back in the vestibule that Nelson and Charlie were able to extract themselves from the hurrying funnel of people.

"What the hell does that mean?" demanded Nelson.

Charlie considered the question.

"It means," he said, "that there won't be a trial."

"I don't understand," protested the broker.

"No," admitted Charlie. "Neither do I. Not yet."

Suddenly it seemed that there was going to be very little difference between what he was attempting to do now and what he had done in the past. Would he still be as good? he wondered.

The photograph of Charlie Muffin was passed slowly around the inner council, then finally returned to the chairman.

"Such a nondescript man," said the chairman.

"Yes," agreed Chiu.

"Incredible."

"Yes," said Chiu again.

"So the insurers aren't as satisfied as the police?"

"Apparently not."

"Such a nondescript man," repeated the chairman, going back to the photograph.

CHAPTER SEVEN

THEIR FORMICA-TOPPED TABLE had been separated from others in the restaurant by wheel-mounted plastic screens trundled squeakily across the bare-boarded floors, and they had sat upon canvas-backed and seated chairs. But the food had been magnificent. It was, decided Charlie, a Chinese restaurant for discerning Chinese.

"It was good?" enquired Jenny Lin Lee anxiously.

"Superb," said Charlie honestly, smiling at her.

She hesitated, then smiled back. A man trained to see through the veils that people erect at first encounters, he was intrigued by the girl. Her frailty was practically waiflike, yet he felt none of the protectiveness that would have been a natural response. Instead, he was suspicious of it, imagining a barrier created with more guile than most people were capable of. A professionalism, in fact. But at what could she be professional? Her hair, obviously very long, was coiled thickly but demurely in a bun at the back of her head. She wore hardly any make-up, just a touch of colour to her lips, and looked more like Nelson's daughter than

49

his mistress. Certainly the broker behaved protectively towards her. But there was another attitude, too. A discomfort, decided Charlie. Definitely a discomfort.

Charlie was aware that he had held back because of his uncertainty, contributing to the awkwardness of the meal.

"Would have tasted better with this," insisted Nelson thickly, raising his minute drinking thimble. Charlie had refused the Mao Tai, preferring beer. Jenny had chosen tea, so the insurance broker had consumed nearly all the bottle.

"Nothing like whisky, though," said Nelson, as if the qualification were necessary. "That's what they call it, you know? Chinese whisky."

"Yes," said Charlie.

"There's no better restaurant in the colony for Peking duck," said Jenny quickly.

She'd realised Nelson's increasing drunkenness and moved hurriedly to take attention from the man. They seemed equally protective towards one another, thought Charlie. It appeared an odd relationship. But then, who was he to judge? He'd never managed a proper relationship in his life. And now he would never have the chance.

"It really was very good," he said.

"It's cooked over charcoal . . . and basted in honey," she said.

"Australia are 160 for five, by the way," said Nelson, adding to his thimble. He looked over the table, grinning apologetically.

"Sorry," he said. "Forgot you're not a cricket fan."

"What are you interested in?" asked Jenny.

Another rescue attempt, thought Charlie.

"Hardly anything," he shrugged.

"There must be *something*," persisted the girl.

Should have been, thought Charlie. Edith's complaint, too. The one he thought he could solve with the appropriated money.

". . . enjoy ourselves now, Edith . . . my money, not yours . . . nothing we can't do. . . ."

Except stay alive. And he'd killed her. By being

bloody stupid. He'd killed her as surely as if he'd pressed the trigger. And he wouldn't forget it, he knew. Not for a single minute of a single day.

"No," said Charlie. "Nothing."

New discomfort grew up between them at the collapse of the conversation, covered within minutes by the arrival of a waiter, clearing dishes and the rotating table centre upon which they had been arranged.

Jenny waited until fresh tea and more cups had been set out and then excused herself, pushing through the screen.

Very little to stay for, thought Charlie.

"Jenny's a very lovely girl," he said dutifully.

"Of course she is," said Nelson.

Charlie frowned, both at the choice of words and the truculence. Nelson was quite drunk.

"Now we've learned about the 12 per cent, I know I'll be dismissed for this damned policy," declared the broker obstinately. He was gazing down into his cup, talking more to himself than to Charlie.

"I've told you . . ." Charlie started, but Nelson talked on unheeding.

". . . and then they'll laugh. Christ, how they'll laugh."

"Who?" demanded Charlie.

"People," said Nelson, looking to him for the first time. "All the people. That's who'll laugh."

"At what, for Christ's sake!"

"Jenny and me . . . but to my face, then. Not like now . . . behind my back."

"But why?"

"Because they consider Robert has strayed outside a well-ordered system."

Charlie turned at the girl's voice. She was standing just inside the screen. She must have realised they had been discussing her, yet she was quite composed, Charlie saw.

"Sorry," mumbled Nelson. "Very sorry . . . just talking . . ."

"I think it's time we left," she said to Nelson. The tenderness in the expression was the first unguarded feeling she had permitted herself all evening, decided Charlie.

"Yes," agreed Nelson, realising he had created an embarrassment. "Time to go home."

He tried to get his wallet from his pocket, but Jenny took it easily from him, settling the bill. She seemed practised in looking after him.

Nelson walked unsteadily between them out into Gloucester Road. There was a taxi at the kerbside and the broker slumped into it, sitting with his head thrown back, eyes closed.

"He doesn't usually drink this much," apologised the girl.

"It doesn't matter," said Charlie.

"Oh, it does," she said urgently. "You mustn't think he's like this all the time. He's not, normally. It's because he's worried about dismissal."

"I know. I've tried to make him understand, but he won't listen."

"It would mean so much for him to be fired."

She didn't appear to believe him either, thought Charlie. What the hell did he have to do to convince them?

"He tried to explain to me back in the restaurant. But it was difficult for him."

She seemed to consider the remark. Then she said, speaking more to herself than to Charlie, "Yes, sometimes it's difficult for him."

"Thank you for the meal," said Charlie, as she started to enter the car. "It was a splendid evening."

She turned at the door, frowning.

"No it wasn't," she said. "It was awful."

On the Kowloon side of the harbour, Harvey Jones stared round his room at the Peninsula Hotel, his body tight with excitement. Specially chosen, the Deputy Director had said. To prove himself. And by Christ, he was going to do just that.

Sure of the security of his locked room, the American took from his briefcase the documents identifying him as an official of the United States Maritime Authority, transferring them to his wallet. A perfect cover for the circumstances, he decided.

It was going to be difficult to sleep despite the jet lag. But he had to rest if he were to perform properly. Carefully he tapped out a Seconal capsule, swilling it down with water from the bedside jug.

He hoped the fire wasn't as straightforward as it appeared. He wanted there to be a startling explanation. Something that would surprise everyone. Impress them, too, when he revealed it.

CHAPTER EIGHT

CLARISSA WILLOUGHBY stared over the dinner table at her husband, throat working with the approach of the predictable anger.

"What do you mean, broke?"

"Just that."

The woman laughed, a disbelieving sound.

"But we can't be."

"For the last two years we've been continuously unlucky," said the underwriter. "It's been nobody's fault."

"It must be somebody's fault," she insisted.

He shook his head, not wanting to argue with her but knowing it was practically unavoidable. It had been ridiculous to expect her understanding, because Clarissa had never understood anything, except perhaps the importance of the Dublin Horse Show compared to Cowes Week or what dress was right for the Royal Enclosure at Ascot but unsuitable for Henley.

"It's a combination of circumstances," he said badly. "Unless we can find something wrong with this ship fire, I can't avoid going down."

"Going down?"

"Bankrupt . . . and struck off the Exchange."

"Oh Christ!"

"I'm sorry."

"Sorry!" she mocked.

"What else do you expect me to say . . . ?"

"There must be something . . . ?"

"I've used all my own money."

"The banks, then . . ."

". . . won't advance another penny."

She thrust up from the table and began jerking about the room. She was very beautiful, he thought. Spoiled and selfish and arrogant, but still very beautiful. And she wasn't a hypocrite, either. She'd never once told him she loved him.

"My friends will laugh at me," she protested.

"Yes," he agreed. "*Your* friends probably will."

He hadn't meant to emphasise the word. She swung back to him.

"What does that mean?"

"It doesn't mean anything," he said wearily.

"Will your friends behave any better?" she demanded. "Do you know anyone you can rely upon?"

Not a friend, accepted Willoughby. Just one man whom the underwriter felt he would never completely understand. He looked up at his wife. How would she react to Charlie Muffin? It would be a cruel experiment; for Clarissa, not Charlie.

"What are you going to do?"

"Delay settlement as long as possible."

"Why?"

"In the hope of there being some reason why we don't have to pay out."

"Is that a possibility?"

He examined the question, slowly shaking his head.

"No," he admitted. "It doesn't seem that it is from what we know so far."

"So you're just trying to put off the inevitable?"

"Yes," he said. "I suppose I am."

"Christ," she said again. "I can hardly believe it."

She lighted a cigarette, puffed nervously at it, and then stabbed it out into an ashtray.

"I'm still finding it difficult," he conceded.

"I want to know, at least a week before," she declared.

"Know what?"

"When the announcement is going to be made about your bankruptcy . . . before all the fuss begins."

"Why?" he asked sadly.

"I would have thought that was obvious."

"Why, Clarissa?" he insisted.

"You surely don't expect me to stay here, in London . . . among all the elbow nudging and sniggering . . . ?"

"I'd hoped you might."

"You should know better than that."

"Yes," he agreed. "Of course I should."

"What a mess," she said. "What a rotten, shitty mess."

"Yes," he said "It is."

She stopped at the table, staring down at him.

"Is that all?"

"All?" he asked.

"All you're going to do? Sit around like a dog that's been beaten once too often and just wait for the final kick?"

"There's nothing more I can do."

"What a man!" she sneered.

"I've said I'm sorry."

"How soon will you hear about the fire?"

"I don't know," he said.

"I won't forgive you for this," she said.

The remark reached through his depression and he laughed at her.

"I don't see anything funny," she said.

"No, darling," said Willoughby. "You wouldn't."

Robert Nelson had become an unconscious weight by the time Jenny manoeuvred him into their apartment. She stumbled with him into the bedroom and heaved him onto the bed. He lay there, mouth open, snoring up at her.

She smiled down.

"Poor darling," she said.

With the expertise of a woman used to handling drunks, she undressed him, rocking him back and forth to free trapped clothing and finally rolling him beneath the covers.

She undressed, hesitated by the bedside and instead put on a kimono, returning to the lounge. The curtains were drawn away from the windows. She slid aside the glass door and went out to the verandah edge, standing with her hands against the rail. Below her the lights of Hong Kong glittered like an overturned jewel box. She looked beyond to where a blackened strip marked the harbour. It was impossible to see the partially submerged liner, but she knew exactly where it would be. She stared towards its unseen shape for a long time, her body still and unmoving.

"Oh Christ," she said at last. It was a sad, despairing sound.

She turned back into the room, her head sunk against her chest, so she was actually inside before she realised it wasn't empty any more. Fright whimpered from her and she snatched her hand up to her mouth. Jenny stood with her back against the cold window, eyes darting to the faces of the three men, seeking identification.

"No," said the eldest of the three. "We're not people you're likely to know."

He spoke Cantonese.

"Oh," she said, in understanding.

"Surprised we are here?"

"Yes."

"Frightened?"

"Yes."

"It's right you should be."

"What do you want?"

"For this stupidity to stop."

"Stupidity?"

"The ship. Don't pretend ignorance."

"What can I do?"

The man smiled.

"That's a naïve question."

"There's nothing I can do," she said desperately.

"What about the man who's come from London?"

"He's supposed to be investigating," she conceded doubtfully.

"And what is he likely to discover?"

"Nothing," she admitted.

"Precisely," said the man. "So he must be shown."

"By me?"

"Who else?"

"How?"

"You're a whore. Used to men. You shouldn't have to ask that question."

There was distaste in the man's voice.

Momentarily she squeezed her eyes closed, to control the emotion.

"You can't make me," she said. It was a pitiful defiance, made more childlike because her voice jumped unevenly.

"Oh, don't be ridiculous," said the man, irritated. He gestured towards the bedroom door beyond which Robert Nelson slept.

"Do you feel for him?"

"I love him," said Jenny. This time she didn't have to force the defiance.

"If you don't do as you are told," said the man quietly, "we will kill him."

Jenny stared across at the leader of the group.

"You do believe me, don't you?" he said.

"Yes," she said. "I believe you."

"So you'll do it?"

"Do I have a choice?"

"Of course not."

Cantonese was the language of another meeting that night, because most of the people assembled in one of the three houses that John Lu owned in Kowloon were street Chinese and uncomfortable with English. It had been right that he should make the announcement, ac-

cording to tradition, so his father had remained in
Hong Kong. Freed of the man's intimidating presence,
the boy had adopted the same cold authority, enjoying
its effect upon the people with him.

"Is that understood?" he demanded.

There were nods and mutterings of agreement.

"Even the New Territories, as well as Kowloon and
Hong Kong," he emphasised.

"We understand," said the man in the front.

"Everyone must know," insisted the millionaire's
son. That was as important as the tradition of making
the announcement.

"They will," promised the man who had spoken earlier.

CHAPTER NINE

CHARLIE HAD EXPECTED his appointment to be cancelled after the court deaths of the two Chinese, but when he telephoned for confirmation, Superintendent Johnson's secretary assured him he was still expected.

Unable to lose the feeling that he was being watched, Charlie walked to police headquarters by a circuitous route, frequently leaving the wider highways to thread through the shop-cluttered alleyways, their incense sticks smouldering against the evil spirits, all the while checking behind and around him and growing irritated when he located nothing and became convinced, yet again, that his instinct had become blunted.

There was another feeling, even stronger than annoyance. He'd always thought of his ability to survive as instinctive, too. It was an attribute he couldn't afford to lose.

"Perhaps I should burn incense," he muttered, recognising the indication of fear.

The police headquarters were as ordered and regimented as the man who commanded them, the regulation spaced decks of the head-bent clerks tidy and unlittered, the offices padded with an almost churchlike hush.

Johnson's office was the model for those outside. Never, decided Charlie as he entered, would it achieve the effect of being occupied and worked in; it was more like an exhibition case.

Even seated behind the predictably imposing desk, Johnson had perfected the stretched-upright gaze of intimidation. The police chief indicated a chair to the left of the desk and Charlie sat, waiting in anticipation.

Almost immediately Johnson looked at his watch, for Charlie to know the pressure upon his time.

"Appointment in thirty minutes," he warned.

"It was good of you to see me so promptly," thanked Charlie. "Especially after what happened in court."

Such men always responded to deference, Charlie knew.

"Murder," confirmed Johnson.

"Murder?"

Johnson would need very little encouragement, guessed Charlie.

"Postmortem examinations proved they both died from a venom-based poison . . . created involuntary lung muscle spasms. Cause of death was asphyxiation."

Charlie said nothing, remembering the strangled breathing.

"The Chinese farm snakes, you know. For food."

"I know," said Charlie.

"So venom is freely available in the colony. . . . Chinese doctors even use it in some cases as health remedies. It'll take more tests, but we think it was either from a Banded Krait or a Coral Snake."

"You said murder," reminded Charlie.

Johnson leaned back in the chair, refusing to be hurried despite his own restriction upon time.

"Know what solves crime?" he demanded.

"What?" asked Charlie. Had Johnson always been as overbearing as this? he wondered. Or developed the attitude since he arrived in the colony?

"Routine. Just simple routine. Finding those responsible for the fire was merely a matter of gradually working through those Chinese employed on the refit, matching the fingerprints to those we found all over the sprinkler systems, and the incendiary devices and then confronting them with the evidence. Simple, logical routine."

"And now you've made an arrest for their murder?" said Charlie.

Johnson shifted, off-balanced by the question.

"Employing the same principle, we've satisfied ourselves we know the man responsible. We've eliminated every person who had contact with the dead men except one."

"Who?"

"A prison cook, Ideally placed to introduce the poison. His name is Fan Yung-ching."

"But you haven't made an arrest?"

"Not yet."

"Because he's returned to mainland China?" suggested Charlie.

Johnson frowned at the anticipation.

"That's what we strongly suspect," admitted the police chief. "We've established that he disappeared from his lodgings and that his family have always lived in Hunan, on the mainland. Apparently he crossed about six months ago."

"I'm surprised how easy it appears to be to go back and forth over the border," said Charlie.

The superintendent leaned forward on his desk, always alert for criticism.

Basically unsure of himself, judged Charlie.

"It's virtually impossible for us to control or even estimate the number that cross each year," conceded the police chief. "At least five thousand come in without Chinese permission, swimming across the bay. Double that number must enter with official approval."

"Ten thousand!" said Charlie.

"Would it frighten you to know that the majority of Chinese crews on British warships and naval support vessels come from communist China, with merely accommodation addresses here to satisfy the regulations about their being Hong Kong Chinese?"

"Yes," admitted Charlie. "It probably would."

"It's a fact," insisted Johnson. "And it frightens the Americans, too. Particularly during joint NATO exercises."

"So you're convinced that the men who destroyed the *Pride of America* were infiltrated into the colony. Then killed by another Chinese agent?"

Johnson nodded, tapping another file neatly taped in red binding at the corner of his desk. The word "closed" was stencilled on it.

"To save the embarrassment that might have come out during the trial," the policeman confirmed.

Johnson had a pigeon-hole mind, decided Charlie.

"Once we confronted the two with the evidence of the fingerprints and the incendiary devices, they made full statements," continued Johnson. "Admitted they were told to cross, then wait until they were contacted ... what espionage people call being ..."

He hesitated, losing the expression.

Sleepers, you bloody fool, thought Charlie. He said nothing. His feet were beginning to hurt and he wriggled his toes, trying to become more comfortable.

". . . I forget the term," dismissed Johnson. "Anyway, they were eventually contacted, given the materials to cause the fire and did what they were told."

"Just as you think the prison cook did?"

Again Johnson looked curiously at the doubt in Charlie's voice.

"From other people at the man's lodging house, we know that the night before the remand hearing another Chinese came to see him. That he handed the cook a package and that afterwards the man seemed agitated and frightened. . . . We've got fingerprints from his room which match those on the rice bowls from which the men ate before they came to court. . . ."

"And that, together with his mainland background, fits neatly into the pattern?"

"I've considered all the evidence," defended Johnson.

"I've seen most of it," reminded Charlie.

"And mine is the proper conclusion on the facts available."

"But doesn't it seem just a little clumsy?" asked Charlie.

"Clumsy?"

"The two who fired the liner were opium smokers, weren't they?" asked Charlie, recalling the indications at the court hearing.

"There was medical evidence to that effect," admitted Johnson. "Many Chinese are."

"And almost illiterate?" pressed Charlie.

"There was no education, no," conceded Johnson.

"What about the cook?"

"Apparently he smoked, too. We haven't been able to establish his literacy, obviously."

"Then to use your guidelines, it's not logical, is it?" said Charlie. "Or even sensible?"

"What?" demanded Johnson, resenting the argument.

"In a fanfare of publicity," said Charlie, "one of the world's most famous passenger liners is brought here; and a man renowned for years of anti-communist preaching announces that it's to become a prestige university at which he's going permanently to lecture against the Peking regime. . . ."

". . . I'm aware of the facts . . ." interrupted Johnson.

". . . Then don't you think it is odd," seized Charlie, "that a country which decides to stifle that criticism—a country which according to you can without the risk of interception move ten thousand people into this colony and therefore, presumably, include in that figure the most expert sabotage agents in any of its armed forces—should select for the task three near-illiterate, drug-taking Chinese whose capture or discovery was practically a foregone conclusion? And by so doing guarantee worse publicity than if it had let the damned ship remain . . . ?"

Johnson laughed, a dismissive sound.

"A logical argument . . ." he began.

". . . Routine logic," interposed Charlie.

". . . Which regrettably doesn't fit the facts," refused Johnson. "You must defer to my having a great deal more knowledge of these matters than you."

"But they just *wouldn't* do it, would they?" insisted Charlie, feeling the caution that he had with Nelson at the danger of his experience being questioned.

"Give me an alternative conclusion," said Johnson.

"At the moment I don't have one," said Charlie. "But I'm going to keep my mind a great deal more open than yours until I've better proof."

"And you think you're going to get that in Hong Kong?" sneered Johnson, carelessly patronising.

"I am going to try."

The large man rose from his desk, staring from the window.

"You're a Westerner," he said, turning back into the room after a few moments. "A round-eye . . . even if there were anything more to discover, which I don't believe there is, you wouldn't stand a cat in hell's chance of penetrating this society."

The second time he'd had that warning in forty-eight hours, calculated Charlie. It was becoming boring.

"And if I can?"

Johnson shook his head at the strange conceit from the unkempt man sitting before him.

"Come back to me with just one piece of produceable evidence that would give me legal cause to reopen the case and I will," he promised. "Just one piece."

He hesitated.

"But I tell you again," he added, "you're wasting your time."

The 12 per cent premium wasn't evidence, decided Charlie. Not without the reason to support it. It could wait until another meeting. And Charlie was sure that there would be one.

"Have you asked the Chinese authorities for any assistance in locating the cook?" asked Charlie.

"There's been a formal application," said Johnson. "But we don't expect any assistance. There never is."

"So what will happen?"

"We'll issue an arrest warrant. And perhaps a statement."

"And there the matter will lie . . . still a communist-inspired fire?"

Johnson smiled, condescending again.

"Until we receive your surprise revelation, there the matter will lie," he agreed. "Irrefutably supported by the facts. There's no way you can avoid a settlement with Mr. Lu."

On the evidence available, decided Charlie, the policeman was right. Poor Willoughby, he thought.

He saw Johnson look again at his watch and anticipated the dismissal, rising from his chair.

"Thank you again," he said.

"Any further help," said Johnson, overgenerous in his confidence, "don't hesitate to call."

"I won't," promised Charlie.

Superintendent Johnson's next appointment was approaching along the corridor as Charlie left. Politely, Charlie nodded.

Harvey Jones returned the greeting.

Neither man spoke.

The telex message awaiting Charlie at the hotel said contact was urgent, so he booked the telephone call to Rupert Willoughby's home. The underwriter answered immediately, with no sleep in his voice.

"Well?" he said. The anxiety was very obvious.

"It doesn't feel right," said Charlie.

"So we can fight?"

The hope flared in the man's voice.

"Impressions," qualified Charlie. "Not facts."

"I can't contest a court hearing on impressions," said Willoughby, immediately deflated. "And according to our lawyers, that's what we could be facing if we prolong settlement."

"I know that," said Charlie. "There is one thing."

"What?"

"Lu agreed to pay you 12 per cent premium. . . ."

". . . I told you that."

"I know. What's your feeling at learning everyone else only got 10 per cent?"

There was no immediate response from the underwriter.

"That doesn't make sense," he said at last. "We were the biggest insurers, after all."

"Exactly."

"So there *is* something more than impressions?" said Willoughby eagerly. Again the hope was evident.

"It's not grounds for refusing to pay," insisted Charlie.

"But what about the court deaths?"

"The police chief is convinced he's solved that . . . and that it doesn't alter anything."

"What about the 12 per cent, linked with the deaths?"

"I didn't tell him about the premiums," admitted Charlie.

"Why the hell not?"

"Because there *is* no link. So I want to understand it, first."

"We haven't the time," protested Willoughby.

"How long?"

"A week at the very outside," said the underwriter.

"That's not enough."

"It'll have to be."

"Yes," accepted Charlie. "It'll have to be."

"Have you seen Lu?"

"Not yet."

"Surely he's the one to challenge about the 12 per cent?"

"Of course he is."

"Well?"

"By itself, it's not enough!" Charlie insisted.

"So what are you going to do?"

"I don't know," admitted Charlie.

"That's not very reassuring."

"I'm not trying to be reassuring. I'm being honest."

"I'd appreciate forty-eight-hour contact," said Willoughby.

And spend the intervening time working out figures on the backs of envelopes and praying, guessed Charlie.

"I'll keep in touch," he promised.

"I'm relying on you," said Willoughby.

Charlie replaced the receiver, turning back upon it almost immediately.

"Damn," he said. He'd forgotten to ask Willoughby to send a letter to Robert Nelson, assuring him of his job. Not that the promise would matter if he didn't make better progress than he was so far. He'd still do it, though. The next call would be soon enough.

He was at the mobile bar, using it for the first time, when the bell sounded. Carrying his drink, he went to the door, concealing his reaction when he opened it.

"I thought you'd be surprised," said Jenny Lin Lee, pouting feigned disappointment. Then she smiled, openly provocative; the hair, which the previous night she had worn so discreetly at the nape of her neck, loose now. She shook her head, a practised movement, so that it swirled about her like a curtain.

"I am," said Charlie.

"Then you're good at hiding things," she said, moving past him into the suite without invitation.

"Perhaps we both are," said Charlie.

Clarissa stood looking at her husband expectantly, when Willoughby put the phone down.

"Nothing," he said, shaking his head. "Some inconsistencies, but nothing that positively helps."

"But the court murders."

"It doesn't change anything, apparently."

"How good is this man you've got there, for Christ's sake?"

The underwriter paused at the question. He knew little more than what he had heard from his father, he realised. Certainly the escape in which Charlie had involved him had been brilliantly organised. But then Charlie had been fighting for his own existence, not somebody else's.

"Very good, I understand," he said.

"Little proof of it, so far," complained the woman.

That was the trouble, thought Willoughby. Proof.

"Give him time," he said unthinkingly.

"I thought that was what we didn't have."

"No," admitted the underwriter. "We don't."

"You won't forget, Rupert, will you?"

"No," he promised. "I won't forget."

"A week's warning, at least."

"A week's warning," he agreed. Why was it, he wondered, that he didn't feel distaste for this woman?

CHAPTER TEN

JENNY LIN LEE had pulled her hair forward and, because she sat with her legs folded beneath her, it practically concealed her body. He was still able to see that, beneath the white silk cheongsam, she was naked.

She took the glass from him, taking care that their hands touched.

"I got the impression last night that you didn't drink," he said.

"Robert needs a sober guardian."

"Where is he now?"

"At the weekly dinner of the businessmen's club," said Jenny disdainfully. "One of the few places that will still let him in."

Purposely she moved her hair aside, so that more of her body was visible. She looked very young, he thought.

"There are some that don't?" he asked.

"Apparently." She shrugged, an uncaring gesture.

"Why?"

"You mean he didn't tell you?" she demanded,

revolving the glass so that the ice clattered against the sides.

"Tell me what?"

"The great embarrassment of Robert Nelson's life," she intoned, deepening her voice to a mock announcement. "He's in love with a Chinese whore."

It was an interesting performance, thought Charlie. So it *had* been a professionalism he'd recognised the previous night. Why, he wondered, had it been so difficult for him to identify? He of all people. Not that he would have used the word to describe her. Because she wasn't. Not like the girl in front of him.

"*. . . Say hello to your uncle, Charlie. . . . There's a good boy. . . . What's your name again, love . . . ?*"

But not a whore. Never have called her that. Not now. She hadn't even taken money, not unless it was offered her. And only then if the rent were due or the corner store were refusing any more credit or there was some new school uniform needed. And she would always describe it as a loan. Actually put scribbled IOU's in the Coronation mug on the dresser. He'd found fifty there, when his mother had died. All carefully dated. And dozens more in the biscuit tin, the one in which she put the rent money and the hire-purchase installments. One of the names, he supposed, had been that of his father. She wouldn't have known, of course. Not for certain. She would have been able to remember them all, though. Because to her they hadn't been casual encounters. None of them.

He didn't believe she'd wanted physical love. Not too much, anyway. It was just that in her simple, haphazard way, she couldn't think how else it would enter, except through the bedroom door.

She'd tried to explain, pleading with him. She'd been crying and he'd thought the mascara streaks had looked like Indian warpaint.

He'd been the National Service prodigy then. Transferred because of his brilliance as an aerial photographer for RAF intelligence to the department that Sir Archibald was creating.

And so very impressed with the accents and the attitudes of the university entrants. Impressed with everything, in fact. And so anxious to belong. He hadn't challenged them, of course. Not yet. That had been the time when he was still trying to ape their talk and their habits, unaware of their amusement.

And been frightened that the sniffling, sobbing woman, who didn't even have the comfort now of any more uncles, would endanger his selection because of the security screening he knew was taking place.

"*. . . can't you understand what it's like to be lonely, Charlie . . . to want somebody you can depend on . . . who won't notice when you're getting old. . . .*"

He'd grimaced at the mascara. And called her ugly. The one person who could have given her the friendship she'd wanted, he thought. And he hadn't understood. Any more than he'd understood what Edith had wanted from him until it was too late. Why had he never been able to dream Edith's dreams?

How long, he wondered, would it take Robert Nelson?

"Strayed outside the well-ordered system," he quoted.

She nodded.

"The Eleventh Commandment," said Jenny. "Thou shalt fuck the natives but not be seen doing it."

"And you don't love him?"

"What's love got to do with being a whore?"

"Very little."

"He's convenient," she said. "And the bed's clean."

"Do you really despise him?"

"I despise being paraded around to garden parties where people won't talk to me and to clubs where I'm ignored, so he can show me off like someone who's recovered from a terminal illness."

"Why don't you tell him that?"

"I have. He says I'm imagining it and he wants me to be accepted."

"Why not leave?"

"Like I said," she sniggered. "The bed's clean. And the money is regular."

"But not enough?"

"There's never enough money . . . that's one of Lucky Lu's favourite expressions."

Charlie slowly lowered himself into a chair facing the girl, feeling the first tingle of familiar excitement.

"I hadn't heard that," he encouraged.

"You'd be amazed, with all the publicity, of the things people haven't heard about Lucky Lu."

The entry into the society that everyone said would be denied him? Charlie frowned. He'd always suspected things that came too easily.

"Like what?" he prompted.

"You got money?" asked the girl.

"As much as you want," offered Charlie, misunderstanding the demand.

She stood, smiling.

"You spend a lot and you get a lot," she promised, walking towards the bedroom.

Charlie remained crouched forward in the chair, momentarily confused. Before Edith's death, there had been many affairs, the sex sometimes as loveless as that being offered by the woman who had disappeared into the bedroom. But for almost two years there had been a celibacy of grief. He'd always known it would end. But not like this. Mechanically almost. But she had hinted a knowledge about Lu of which even Nelson seemed unaware—a knowledge he'd never learn if he rejected her.

"I don't believe you can reach from there," she called.

He winced at the awkward coarseness, then stood hesitantly, walking towards the bedroom. There was nothing, he realised. No lust. No feeling. Certainly not desire. Just apprehension.

She'd discarded the cheongsam and was sitting back on her heels, near the top of the bed. She'd swept her hair forward again, covering herself except for her breasts, which pouted through like pink-nosed puppies.

"You only keep your clothes on for short time. You don't want a short time, do you?"

Rehearsed words, he thought. Like prompt cards in a child's classroom. Would his mother have ever been like this? No, he decided. She wouldn't have even *known* the expression. He was sure she wouldn't.

Reluctantly he took off his jacket and tie, edging onto the bed.

"What do you know about Lu?" he said. He wouldn't be able to make love to her, he knew.

She put her hand on his thigh, feeling upwards, then gazing at him, pulling her mouth into an artificially mournful expression.

"That's not very flattering for a girl," she complained. Immediately there was the prostitute's smile.

"We'll soon improve that," she promised.

She moved her hand up, reaching through his shirt, then stopped.

"What's that?"

Charlie looked down.

"String vest," he said.

"A what!"

"String vest. Supposed to keep you cool in hot weather."

"Good God!"

She began to laugh, genuinely now and he smiled with her.

"Doesn't seem to work, either."

"Let me see," she insisted.

Feeling foolish, he took off his shirt and she began to laugh even more, pointing at him with outstretched finger and rocking backwards and forwards on her heels.

"You look ridiculous," she protested. "Like a fish ... a fish, wrapped up inside a net."

He did, thought Charlie. A flat fish. Very apt.

He reached for her outstretched hand, intending to repeat the question about Lu, then realised that the amusement had changed, becoming more strident, edging towards hysteria.

"... What ...?" he began and then saw she was crying, her eyes flooded with emotion.

"Oh fuck," she said, desperately. "Fuck, fuck, fuck. ..."

She pumped her hand in his, in her frustration and

then came forward, pressing her face into his shoulder. Charlie put his arms around her, holding her against him. Her skin was very smooth and he could feel her tipped, soft breasts against him. There was still no reaction within him.

"It was a good try," he said quietly. Normally there was anger at realising he had been wrong. This time it was relief.

She sobbed on.

"Why?" he said.

"Robert's so worried . . ." she said, her voice uneven and muffled against his shoulder. "He's convinced he'll be dismissed, because of the premium. . . ."

"But why this?"

She pulled away from him.

"I'm sorry," she said.

"It wouldn't have worked."

"I could have pretended . . . whores do all the time."

"I couldn't."

It was a sad smile, but controlled now.

"No," she said. "You couldn't, could you?"

"I still want to know why."

"Wanted to compromise you . . . then plead for Robert. Ask you not to recommend that he be fired. Blackmail you even. Another whore's trick."

"He's not going to be sacked," insisted Charlie. "I've told him that, more times than I can count. In a few days, I'll get Willoughby to reassure him by letter."

She was back on her heels now, gazing at him. Crying had puffed her eyes, he saw.

"It's my fault, you know," she blurted suddenly.

"What is?"

". . . The fire . . . everything . . . all because of me."

Charlie leaned forward, taking her hand again.

"Jenny," he said urgently "What are you saying?"

"Lu's people are talking openly to the Chinese about it. . . . They have to, you see. For Lu's family to recover face, it's important that everyone knows. . . ."

"Jenny," he stopped. "Tell me from the beginning, tell me so that I can understand. . . ."

She sniffled and he groped into his pocket for a handkerchief. She kept it in her hand, tracing her fingers over his wrist, a little-girl gesture.

"Lu doesn't just get his money from shipbuilding and property development and oil," she began slowly. "That's crap. . . . Part of the great benefactor publicity machine. . . ."

"What else?"

"He owns a good third of the bars and brothels in Wanchai," announced the girl. "Maybe more. They're quieter, now that the war in Vietnam is over and the Americans aren't coming here, and the Sixth Fleet has gone. But there's still enough business. Not that they matter, by themselves. He's got at least two factories here in Hong Kong manufacturing heroin from the poppy resin that comes in from Thailand and Burma. . . . It's called Brown Sugar, or Number Three. . . ."

She paused, then went on: "He's the biggest supplier in the colony and ships to America and Europe as well. . . ."

Another pause.

"You know what a Triad is?"

"Something like a Chinese Mafia?"

She nodded.

"Lu's a paymaster for at least three Triads, with branches not just here but in Europe as well."

"How do you know all this . . . ?"

She ignored the question.

"And then there's the name—Lucky Lu. It doesn't come from the luck he had on the Hong Kong stock market, like all the publicity says. He runs the casinoes and mah-jong games throughout Hong Kong and Kowloon. . . ."

The sad smile again.

"The Chinese are the biggest gamblers in the world," she said. "Only Lucky Lu is always the winner. . . ."

"How do you know all this?" repeated Charlie. Almost enough to return to Johnson, he decided. He still wanted a link with the 12 per cent premium.

Her head was pressed forward now, so that she didn't have to look at him, and when she spoke her voice was muffled once more.

"Before meeting Robert," she said, "I was with Johnny Lu . . . the son that controls Lucky's vice businesses. . . . I was his number-one woman. . . ."

"I've seen his pictures," said Charlie. "He seems to be almost his father's shadow."

She hesitated.

". . . Johnny told me not to go," she remembered, distantly. "Told me I wouldn't be accepted. . . . He was right. . . ."

"Why was the ship fire your fault?" demanded Charlie.

"Robert didn't get the major share of the insurance because he was better than anybody else," said Jenny. "He got it because Lu planned it that way . . . planned it that the man who took his son's woman and caused the family loss of face would be the greatest sufferer when the ship burned. . . . That's why the premium was higher. . . ."

At last, thought Charlie. It was all so remarkably simple.

"Lu did it himself?"

She shook her head at the naïvety of the question.

"Of course," she said. "If you knew more about the Asian mind, you'd know that loss of face is the worst insult a Chinese can suffer . . . something that's got to be avenged. . . ."

"And having ensured that it wouldn't cost him a penny, he even managed to stage it so that his famous anti-communist campaign would benefit?" he said, in growing awareness.

"Because he is *such* an avowed anti-communist, it made the story even more believable, didn't it?" she said.

"What about the shipyard workers . . . and the prison cook?"

"Chosen because they were mainland refugees," she

said. "Frightened people who'd got deeply into debt at Lu's gambling places and were given the way to settle. . . ."

". . . and as a safeguard against the shipyard men recanting on the rehearsed story, which they would almost certainly have done in court, he had them killed?"

"Yes."

"Why didn't you tell Robert all this?" asked Charlie suddenly. "Why wait so long?"

—"And let him know that the Chinese as well as the European community in Hong Kong were laughing at him for falling in love with a whore? He's suffering enough as it is."

"But it means we can contest the claim. . . . Robert would have realised that. . . ."

"Oh, you poor man," she said. "This is street gossip . . . bar talk. The only proof is the cook, who's probably in Hunan by now. Or dead, like the other two. This isn't anything you can fight Lu with. . . . He's won. Like he always wins."

She was right, realised Charlie. About the proof anyway. He still had nothing.

"I'm buggered if he'll win," said Charlie.

"I told you to show how Robert had been tricked," said the girl. "To show why he shouldn't be fired. Not to fight any court hearing."

"There'll be a way," promised Charlie.

"I'd like to believe that. God, how I'd like to believe that."

Charlie heard the noise first. He spun off the bed, crouched towards the linking door and then remained there, staring up foolishly at the figure of Robert Nelson framed in the doorway.

"Oh no," said the girl quietly. "Dear God, no."

"If you set out to do this sort of thing, you should ensure your corridor doors are secured," said Nelson.

He was striving for enormous dignity, realised Charlie. A nerve twitching high on his left cheek was the only hint of the difficulty he was having in controlling himself.

Charlie motioned towards the now-cowering girl. At last she'd tried to protect herself with the bedcover. She was crying again, he saw, softly this time.

". . . We didn't . . . There was nothing . . ." he started, but the broker talked over him.

"That's not really important, is it?"

"Of course it's important," shouted Charlie. "She came here because she loves you."

"It looks like it."

"Don't be a bloody fool."

"Like the Chinese think of me, as well as everybody else?"

". . . You heard . . ." started Charlie but again Nelson refused him.

". . . Enough. And I'm as determined as you are that Lu won't succeed in his claim."

He looked to the girl.

". . . I don't want you back at the apartment," he said evenly.

". . . Please . . ." she began to plead.

"Just pack your stuff and get out. Tonight."

"For Christ's sake," protested Charlie. "This is ridiculous. What's wrong with you?"

"Nothing," said Nelson. "Not any more. And when I establish that Lu's claim is false, there won't be any more laughter, either."

So Nelson didn't understand. Any more than he'd been able to, all those years ago.

The broker turned away from the bedroom, but Charlie called out, halting him.

"Where are you going?"

"To find one of the Chinese spreading the story she recounted and get him to swear an affidavit incriminating Lu," said Nelson, starting towards the outer door again.

"Stop him," said the girl urgently.

"Robert," yelled Charlie, hurrying into the adjoining room. "That won't work. . . . Wait. We'll go to the police first. . . . They're the people . . ."

Nelson slammed the door without looking around, leaving Charlie standing near the tiny bar.

"Assholes," he said.

She was at the bedroom door when he turned. Because she had only worn the cheongsam, it had taken her seconds to dress. She had stopped crying, but her eyes were still swollen.

"Your handkerchief," she said, holding it out.

"You can keep it if you want."

She shook her head.

"Whores don't cry for long."

She shrugged, a gesture of defeat.

"He expected to catch us," she announced.

"What?"

"Robert. He expected to find us. He never really trusted me . . . thought I couldn't forget the old ways. That's why he came in without knocking . . . always unsure. . . ."

Just as Edith had always been unsure, thought Charlie. Never quite able to believe their marriage was for him anything different from everything else he did, another way of proving himself equal.

"But why me?"

"You'd have been the obvious choice."

"He'll have recovered in the morning," said Charlie hopefully.

Jenny shook her head.

"No," she said simply.

"Where will you go?"

"I'm known in all the bars," she said bitterly.

"Wait. Until tomorrow at least."

"Maybe," she said unconvincingly.

"I'll contact you tomorrow," he said. "After I've seen the police."

She gave him a pitying look.

"You don't stand a chance," she insisted.

"People have been telling me that for as long as I can remember," he said. It was good to feel confident again. It had been a long time. More than two years, in fact. Not since he'd started to run.

Charlie's second telephone call stopped Willoughby as he was leaving his Knightsbridge flat for the City. The underwriter listened without interruption as Charlie repeated what the girl had told him, without naming her as the immediate source.

"Dear God," said Willoughby softly.

"There's still no proof," warned Charlie, immediately detecting the feeling in the other man's voice.

"It would mean we wouldn't have to pay a penny. . . ."

"I said there's no proof."

"But you can get it, surely?"

"I can get the police to investigate. . . . To be produced in court, it will have to be something official."

"Do that then. And Charlie . . ."

"What?"

"Thank you."

There was no way to prick the man's optimism, decided Charlie.

"Something else," he said.

"What?"

"I want you to write a letter to Nelson, assuring him that his job is safe."

"Why?"

"It's important."

The inner council were impressed, realised Chiu Chin-mao, looking around the faces before him.

They had remained unspeaking during the recording of Charlie's bedroom discussion with Jenny Lin Lee, and for those who did not speak sufficient English, Chiu Chin-mao had provided Cantonese transcripts.

"The encounter was excellently monitored," said the chairman, when the tape ended. "Congratulate your people upon installing the devices so well."

"Thank you," said Chiu. "I will."

"So now the Englishman knows the truth?"

"Yes."

"I wonder what action he'll persuade the police to take?"

Chiu knew he wasn't expected to give an opinion and said nothing.

"Why did the girl try to seduce the Englishman?"

asked the chairman suddenly. "Why didn't she just tell him about the fire?"

"I assumed what she said on the recording was the truth . . . that she wanted to compromise him into protecting the employment of the man she's living with," suggested Chiu.

The chairman shook his head.

"Stupid woman," he said. "Will Nelson cause any problems?"

"I've tried to use it to our advantage," said Chiu.

"How?"

"John Lu hasn't the cunning of his father," said Chiu. "I've calculated upon him panicking."

"By doing what?"

"Letting Lu's people know what Nelson is trying to do in the waterfront bars."

"Yes," agreed the chairman. "It can't do any harm."

CHAPTER ELEVEN

CHARLIE WAS STILL in his dressing gown when Superintendent Johnson telephoned.

"I was about to call you," he said, recognising the police chief's voice.

"I'd like to see you," said Johnson.

"When?"

"As soon as possible."

Charlie hesitated. "What for?"

"It had better wait until you get here."

"It sounds formal."

"It is."

"Thirty minutes," promised Charlie.

It took him twenty. The building was still wrapped in its ordered calm as Charlie followed the clerk through the hushed corridor to Johnson's office. This time the man stood as Charlie entered, his manner different from their previous meetings. Johnson pointed to the same chair and Charlie sat down, curious at the man's changed attitude.

"Unpleasant news," announced Johnson bluntly.

"What?"

"Robert Nelson was found by a harbour patrol boat just before dawn this morning. Drowned."

"What!" repeated Charlie, incredulous.

"He's dead, I'm afraid."

"She told me to stop him," remembered Charlie.

"I didn't hear what you said," complained Johnson.

"He was murdered," said Charlie positively.

Johnson spread his hands, shaking his head as he did so.

"Of course it's a shock," he said. "He drowned . . . an accident."

"I don't believe it was an accident," insisted Charlie.

Johnson sighed, annoyance overriding the artificial sympathy. The superciliousness was returning, Charlie realised.

"Any more than you believe what happened to the ship?" demanded the policeman, intending sarcasm.

"I *know* what happened to the ship," said Charlie. "Lu planned its destruction."

"Oh, for God's sake!" rejected Johnson.

"Wait," pleaded Charlie. "Hear me out . . . and then see if you think Nelson still died accidentally."

Johnson settled behind his desk. Predictably he looked at his watch.

Charlie watched the policeman's face as he recounted the story that Jenny Lin Lee had told him, omitting only the circumstances in which Nelson had found them in the hotel suite, but when Johnson did react, it was in a way quite unexpected by Charlie.

The police chief laughed, head thrown back to emphasise his mockery.

"Preposterous," said Johnson. "Utterly and completely preposterous."

". . . But the facts . . ." started Charlie.

"There are *no* facts," crushed Johnson. "Just one small inconsistency—the apparent willingness to pay a premium higher than agreed with the other insurers. But that doesn't prove anything."

"It proves *everything!*"

"Lu is a multimillionaire, unquestionably so," said Johnson. "The insurance money will only just cover the purchase of the *Pride of America*. The money honouring the contracts with the professors and staff he engaged for his university he has had to pay himself, so he's actually *out* of pocket. He'll recover $20,000,000, but will have spent more. Insurance frauds are for profit, not exercise. The 12 per cent would be proof if it showed he had made a profit. And it doesn't."

"But the point is loss of face."

"That's Chinese business," refused Johnson. "You'll get nowhere in this colony trying to prove a crime by invoking folklore and tradition."

"How the hell do you prove a crime in this colony?" demanded Charlie.

Johnson stiffened at the intended rudeness.

"When I took over the running of the police force," he said, speaking slowly, "it was riven by corruption and scandal. I cleaned it up into one of the most honest in the world . . . by strict observance of Home Office regulations. And common sense."

"And common sense dictates that you don't probe too deeply into the affairs of one of the richest and most influential men in Asia?"

"Not when there isn't a good enough reason for so doing," said Johnson. "To operate here, there has to be a balance—knowing when to act and when to withhold. Since I became chief of police, the crime rate has never been so low. I respect the Chinese. And they respect me. It's a working relationship."

"And you'll not instruct your vice squad to probe Lu?"

Johnson shook his head positively.

"I had a crime of arson," he said. "I arrested the culprits, who admitted it in legally recorded statements. The escape of their murderer is an embarrassment, but understandable in the circumstances of Hong Kong. I see no need to launch a meaningless, wasteful investigation."

"What about Robert Nelson's death?"

"There has already been a postmortem examination," said Johnson. "There was nothing besides the water in his lungs that could have caused his death."

"He was murdered," insisted Charlie.

"Your company's representative in this colony was a dissolute . . ." said Johnson.

He hesitated, uncertain whether to continue. Then he said: "There are certain rules by which colonials are expected to live. Unfortunately, Mr. Nelson chose to ignore those rules. By openly cohabitating with a Chinese girl . . . and not just an ordinary Chinese girl at that . . . he cut himself off from both societies."

"I've already had the rules explained to me," broke in Charlie. "You can screw them as long as no one knows and you keep your eyes closed. . . ."

"Don't mock or misquote a system about which you know nothing," said the policeman. "It maintains the status quo of this colony."

"So Nelson was an embarrassment whom no one will really miss?"

"There's no secret that he drank heavily. The medical examination showed an appreciable level of alcohol in his body."

"Oh come on!" jeered Charlie. "Blind drunk, he stumbled into the harbour."

Johnson was making a visible effort to control his annoyance.

"I've no doubt whatsoever that the inquest verdict will be accidental death."

"I'll prove you wrong," promised Charlie determinedly.

"By Chinese folklore and the comic-book ramblings of a Chinese prostitute?" said Johnson. "Isn't it time you simply accepted your liability, settled whatever claim is being made for the loss of the ship, and stopped running around making a fool of yourself?"

Johnson's refusal meant there was no chance of obtaining any official rebuttal of Lu's claim, realised Charlie. And seven thousand miles away a poor bastard was having the first easy day for months and imagined he was safe.

"Please," he tried again, accepting the error of antagonising the other man. "Surely there's sufficient doubt for some sort of investigation?"

"Not in my opinion," said Johnson adamantly.

"Let's not risk the status quo," challenged Charlie, facing the hopelessness of persuading the man.

"No," agreed Johnson, still holding his temper, "let's not."

"Aren't you frightened of pressure from London?" demanded Charlie.

Johnson's face tightened at the threat.

"This colony is self-governing."

"It's a Crown colony, still answerable to Whitehall," said Charlie.

It was a stupid attempt, he recognised. How could he risk going to the London authorities? Even if Willoughby tried, there would be a demand for the underwriter's source. He might be safe in Hong Kong, but he could never sustain a London enquiry.

"If there is any interest from London, I'm sure I can satisfy it," said Johnson.

He'd destroyed any hope of getting assistance from the policeman, decided Charlie. And he could think of no one else.

"Is there anything you want officially done about Nelson?" he asked, anxious now to end the meeting.

"Formal identification."

Unspeaking, Charlie followed the police chief through the cathedral-quiet corridors and into the basement. He'd been too often in mortuaries. And never been able to inure himself to the surroundings. The habitual casualness of the attendants offended him, as did the identification tags, always tied like price tickets to the toes.

The drawer was withdrawn and the sheet pulled aside. At last Robert Nelson had lost the expression of permanent anxiety.

"Yes," said Charlie.

"What about his clothes?" asked an attendant, as Charlie turned to leave.

Charlie looked back. The man was indicating a jumble of sodden clothing visible inside a transparent plastic bag.

"I'll send for it," said Charlie. The bundle had been tied together in the Eton tie, he saw.

Jenny opened the door of Nelson's apartment hurriedly, the hope discernible in her face.

"Oh," she said. There was disappointment in her voice.

"I'm glad you stayed," said Charlie.

"I promised," she said. "But he isn't here."

"I knew he wouldn't be."

She stood aside for him to enter.

"What's happened?" she anticipated, remaining by the door.

"He's dead, Jenny."

She nodded.

"Of course," she said.

She shrugged. "I tried so hard to protect him. That's all I wanted to do, stop him getting hurt."

"In the harbour," said Charlie, inadequately. "Drowned."

She was standing very still, refusing any emotion.

"It'll be thought an accident," she said.

"Yes," he said. "That's how they're treating it."

"But he was murdered, of course."

"I know."

"I wonder which of them did it?" she said. She spoke quietly to herself.

"Which of them?" demanded Charlie.

She looked directly at him, as if considering her words.

"Nothing," she said finally.

"What is it, Jenny?"

"Nothing," she said again.

"Help me," pleaded Charlie.

"I tried," she said sadly. "For nothing. So no more mistakes."

She paused.

"Poor Robert," she said. "Poor darling."

"I'll make the arrangements," said Charlie.

"Yes."

"I'm sorry, Jenny. Really sorry."

She made a listless movement. The resignation was almost visible, decided Charlie.

"Did you tell the police about the fire?" she asked.

"They didn't believe me," said Charlie.

"So nothing is going to be done about that, either?"

"Not by the police, no."

"I told you," she reminded him. "I told you Lu would win. He always does."

"I'll upset it," said Charlie. "Some way I'll upset it."

"No, you won't," she said. "You'll just get hurt. Like Robert. And like me."

"Do you want me to stay?"

She looked at him curiously.

"Stay?"

"Here, for a while."

She shook her head.

"I told you before," she said. "Whores don't cry for long."

"Why keep calling yourself that?" said Charlie angrily.

"Because that's how I've always been treated," she said. "And how I always will."

When Charlie got back to the hotel, he found there had been three attempts to contact him from London by telephone.

"And there's been a telex message," added the receptionist.

Remaining at the desk, Charlie tore open the envelope.

LU TODAY ISSUED HIGH COURT WRITS, it said. It was signed by Willoughby.

Charlie had started towards the lift, head still bent over the message, when he felt the hand upon his arm.

"I've been waiting for you," said the man. "Gather you're as interested in the ship fire as I am."

"Who are you?" asked Charlie, recognising the accent and feeling the immediate stir of anxiety deep in his stomach.

"Harvey Jones," said the man, offering his hand. "United States Maritime Authority."

My ass, thought Charlie instinctively. And this time, he knew, there was nothing wrong with his instinct.

"It was never part of the original proposal," protested Lu. As always, he spoke quietly, despite his anger.

"It was an over-reaction," admitted his son. His habitual nervousness was even more pronounced.

"Which you could have prevented."

"I'm sorry."

"You're stupid," said Lu. "Is there a risk of the police treating it as murder?"

"There's been no announcement. It was done carefully."

"The absence of an announcement doesn't mean anything."

"I know."

"So you've permitted an uncertainty."

"Yes."

"Do you know what would have happened to anyone who wasn't my son?"

"Yes."

"And even that wouldn't be an obstacle if it became a choice between us."

"I know."

"There mustn't be any more mistakes."

"There won't be."

"I'm determined there won't," assured Lu. "Quite determined."

CHAPTER TWELVE

CHARLIE WAS FORCING the calmness, sitting deep into the chair with his hands outstretched along the armrests, watching Harvey Jones pace the room.

Trapped, Charlie decided. Not quite as positively as he had been beside Sir Archibald's grave. Or during the chase that had followed. But it was close. Too close. And all his own fault. He hadn't considered it properly, realising the obvious American reaction to the possibility of communist China deliberately destroying something so recently U.S. property.

He'd managed to conceal the nervousness churning through him, Charlie knew. But only just. The American was already worryingly curious. Otherwise he wouldn't have stage-managed the lobby meeting. So it would only take one mistake. And Jones would isolate it. Charlie was sure of that, because he'd determined the American was good. Bloody good. Which meant he had to be better. A damned sight better.

So far, he had been. With the caution of a poacher tickling a trout into the net, Charlie had put out the lures. And Jones had taken them. But even then it had needed all Charlie's experience to spot the tradecraft in the other man. For him, Charlie felt the respect of one professional for another. He hesitated at the thought. A professional wouldn't have allowed the miscalculation which had brought about this meeting, he decided.

"I'd have expected someone with Johnson's experience to see the bit that doesn't fit," suggested Jones.

"What was that?" asked Charlie. He would have to be cautious of apparently innocent questions. Cautious of everything.

"That Peking would hardly have used ignorant hopheads for a job like this."

"Johnson told you?"

Jones completed a half circuit of the room. The movement was as much of a test as the questions, Charlie recognised; an attempt to irritate him by its very theatricality.

"Made a joke of it," said the American, inviting some annoyed response.

"Johnson seems to think almost everything I say is amusing," said Charlie.

"Oh?"

Shit, thought Charlie. He had to continue.

"I asked him today to investigate what I really think happened to the *Pride of America*," he said, covering the awkwardness. Perhaps volunteering Jenny's story wouldn't be so much of a mistake. Jones would become suspicious of obvious evasion.

"And what do you think really happened?"

"That Lu planned the fire. And the destruction of the ship."

"What!"

Jones eased into a facing chair, halted by the announcement.

Again leaving out the girl's attempted seduction, Charlie recounted the story. He was getting very adept at it, he thought. To tell Jones could be another lure, rather than a mistake. The man's reaction would be a further confirmation. Not that he really needed it.

"Jesus!" said Jones.

"Clever, isn't it?" said Charile.

"But how the hell can you prove it?"

The man had failed, thought Charlie. If Jones really had represented the U.S. Maritime Authority, he'd have been as interested in proving it as Charlie. And accepted it as a joint operation. Jones would realise the mistake and recover quickly, he guessed.

"I can't prove it," admitted Charlie.

"Johnson isn't interested?"

"Called it preposterous."

"Which it is."

Clever, assessed Charlie. Now he was forced to talk further, always with the risk of a slip.

"But it fits better with opium-smoking illiterates," he pointed out.

"That really was damned smart of you," repeated Jones.

The American was still manipulating the conversation, Charlie accepted.

"It seems obvious," he said uneasily.

"Not to Johnson who's supposed to be the expert."

"He's got a policeman's mind . . . trained only to accept fact."

"What are you trained in?" demanded Jones openly.

"Trying to avoid £6,000,000 settlements," said Charlie.

Jones smiled.

Amusement? wondered Charlie. Or admiration at escaping again? There was as much danger in showing himself an expert in this type of interrogation as there was in a misplaced word.

The American rose, to pace the room once more.

He went towards the bar and Charlie said, "Would you like a drink?"

"Never touch it," refused Jones.

Because it might blur his faculties, no matter how slightly, guessed Charlie. And he judged Jones to be the sort of man who didn't like to lose control of anything, most of all himself. About him there was an overwhelming impression of care. It was most obvious in the pressed and matched clothes, but extended to the manicured hands and close-cropped hair and even to the choice of cologne that retained his just-out-of-the-bathroom freshness.

"Can I help you to one?" offered the American.

"No," said Charlie. Jones didn't want to impair his thinking, he reflected. And he couldn't afford to.

"Thought about asking for an independent autopsy?" asked Jones. "If you could discover any injury to Nelson inconsistent with his being drowned, it would be something upon which Johnson would have to act."

An invitation to reveal his expertise, saw Charlie, the apprehension tightening within him.

"No," he said. "I hadn't thought of that."

"Might be an idea," said Jones.

"Yes," agreed Charlie. "It might."

"How much time do you think you have, now that Lu's issued writs?" asked Jones, nodding to Willoughby's telex message that lay between them on the table.

He'd endangered the underwriter by letting the American read the cable as they had travelled up in the lift, realised Charlie belatedly. It had been a panicked reaction to gain time. Now unless he allayed the uncertainties, it would be automatic for Jones to have their London bureau check Willoughby. And in his present state, the underwriter wouldn't be able to satisfy any enquiry.

"Not much," said Charlie. "Our lawyers will want to begin preparing an answer to Lu's claim almost immediately. And they won't be able to do that on what I've got available."

"So you're in trouble?"

But just how much? wondered Charlie.

"Looks like it," he said.

"I'll be intrigued to see what you do," said Jones.

"What would you do?" demanded Charlie, turning the question.

Jones made an uncertain movement.

"I'm in a more fortunate position than you," he said. "There's no money riding on what I do."

"What then?" insisted Charlie.

Jones was at the window. He turned at the open question.

"Just a group of government officials who want to know if Peking put a match to a ship so recently American property."

Now Jones was making mistakes, thought Charlie, as the different confirmation came of his earlier assessment. Or was he? Perhaps it was an invitation to Charlie to become more careless.

"Why should that interest them?" he pressed. "The sale had gone through, after all."

"But only just," said Jones. "Hardly be a friendly act towards America, would it?"

"And that worries a shipping authority sufficiently to send you all the way here?"

"You'd better believe it," said Jones glibly.

But I don't, thought Charlie. It would be wrong to let the disbelief be too obvious.

"So what are *you* going to do?" he repeated. It was time to attempt some insurance of his own. Or at least as much protection as possible.

Jones returned to his chair, apparently accepting the failure of his wanderings to irritate Charlie.

"Like you, I'm stuck with the official version," said the American.

"But I don't accept it. What about you?"

"I like your story better than Johnson's," conceded Jones.

"Why not ask Johnson's help?" suggested Charlie. "He might change his mind if he got a second request so quickly."

Jones made a dismissive gesture with his well-kept hands.

"He'd know it originated from you. And he didn't strike me as a man prepared to change his mind very often."

"Perhaps you're right," said Charlie. About now, he decided.

"We could work together," said Jones, promptly on cue.

Charlie maintained his relaxed pose, smiling across at the other man. He'd realised his earlier mistake.

"You're welcome to anything I learn," promised Charlie. "And if you come up with anything, I'd like to know about it."

"I was actually thinking of something closer," said Jones.

I know you were, thought Charlie. Aloud, he said, "I was never much for teamwork."

"We could both benefit," Jones argued.

He already had, Charlie decided. Having led Jones into making the suggestion, then rejecting it, he would know from the closeness of the man's attention just how strong Jones's uncertainty of him remained. Which was the maximum insurance for which he could hope.

"Or get in each other's way," said Charlie. "I think it's better we work independently. But perhaps exchange what we come up with."

"So you're a loner?"

"Every time."

"How many times have there been?"

"What?" said Charlie, momentarily confused by the question.

"How long have you worked for insurance companies?"

"Must be twenty years," assured Charlie, wanting to change position in the chair but knowing the other man would recognise the nervousness it would betray.

"Long as that?"

"Hardly entrust a £6,000,000 investigation to a newcomer, would they?"

"Not unless he had particular qualities . . . like being able to see something that the police don't regard as unusual."

"Seemed obvious, like I told you."

"Sure," agreed Jones. "You told me."

Charlie waited, but the American didn't continue. The man was letting the silence build up, trying to disturb him as he had attempted with the pointless meandering around the suite.

Remembering the way the encounter had been forced upon him, to *become* annoyed would be entirely natural, realised Charlie, just in time.

"Right," he said positively, standing up. "If there's nothing more with which I can help you at the moment..."

". . . If you're quite sure there isn't?" interrupted Jones, making his most direct approach since they had begun talking.

". . . and I have a funeral to arrange," continued Charlie, refusing to respond to the innuendo.

Once more Jones stood, accepting his dismissal.

"Kind of you to let me barge in like this."

"No trouble at all," said Charlie.

"We'll keep in touch."

"Of course."

"I'm at the Peninsula."

"I'll remember that."

"Damned clever of you, seeing the flaw in Johnson's case," reiterated Jones, shaking his head in feigned admiration and wanting to prolong the meeting as long as possible.

Now it was Charlie's turn to use silence.

"I'll get along then," said Jones finally.

"Yes," encouraged Charlie.

Charlie stood unmoving for several moments after the door had closed behind the American. Then he went to the bar. The bottle vibrated against the glass edge as he splashed the whisky out, drank it in one gulp, then poured a second.

Good, he judged. But good enough? There was no way he could be sure. Certainly Jones had been pressing until the very end. But it would be wrong to read too much into that. It was basic procedure: the sort of persistence he would have shown himself in the same circumstances.

He paused at the thought. As frightened as he had been, there had been something enervating about the confrontation. Perhaps the feeling of a matador facing an insufficiently weakened bull and knowing it could kill him. Charlie snorted, disgusted with himself. That was melodramatic bullshit, he thought.

He was not fighting bulls. He was fighting for his life. Again.

He wanted to run. The awareness came suddenly, surprising him. He was no more prepared to die than he had been on the East Berlin border or during the pursuit by the Americans or British or during any of the missions upon which he'd been sent by the underwriter's father.

A man who relied so much upon instinct, Charlie recognised his determination to survive as the strongest force within him.

So how *could* he survive? Certainly not by running. That would provide whatever confirmation Jones needed and start the chase all over again. Resolve everything quickly then. Far quicker than Willoughby was demanding. But how, against Johnson's official refusal to reopen the case?

"You're fucked, Charlie," he told himself. "Without even being kissed."

He booked the call to London, stared at his glass, considering another drink and then rejected the idea. It never helped.

Willoughby's response was immediate. The man must spend all his time waiting by the telephone, thought Charlie.

"Nelson's dead," announced Charlie, quietening a flurry of questions from the underwriter.

"Oh God," said Willoughby.

"Yes."

"What happened?"

It took Charlie only a few moments to tell the underwriter. Hardly long enough, he thought. A man's life dismissed in a minute or two.

"And Johnson still won't help?" demanded Willoughby, when Charlie had finished.

"Not upon anything. And to be fair to the man, I don't suppose there's any logical, police reason why he should."

"But you said . . ."

". . . that I didn't have any proof," reminded Charlie. If Harvey Jones instituted any investigation in London, Willoughby would collapse, thought Charlie again.

"I haven't much more time," said the underwriter, defeat etched into his voice. "I'll have to make an announcement soon."

Perhaps neither of us have got much more time, thought Charlie.

"I realise that," he said.

"What about Nelson trying to prove the girl's story?" said Willoughby desperately. "That's a motive . . . cause enough for some sort of police investigation. That and the premium . . . ?"

"But there's no evidence of what Nelson was trying to do . . . apart from my word. Death was by drowning. And he'd been drinking."

"So there's still nothing with which we can dispute the writs?"

"Not yet."

"I was very hopeful."

"I warned you not to be."

"It just seemed so good. . . ."

The broker's death registered fully for the first time.

"Poor Robert," said Willoughby. "Christ, what a disaster."

"There's something else," said Charlie.

He had to warn Willoughby of the danger of Harvey Jones, he knew.

Charlie had expected alarm, but it was more hopeless resignation in the underwriter's voice when he had finished telling of the American's visit.

"You could be wrong," said Willoughby. "He really could be employed by the Maritime agency."

"No chance," said Charlie, refusing Willoughby any false reassurance despite his awareness of the man's need. "I've spent all my life seeing people like Harvey Jones for what they really are."

"And he suspects you?"

"Of course not. At the moment he's just curious."

"But why?"

"He's trained to spot inconsistencies. And he saw it

straightaway in the official account, just like I did. It's only natural he should wonder about someone who thinks like he does."

"What the hell are we going to do, Charlie?"

"I don't know."

"Get out," insisted Willoughby suddenly. "All you can do is run."

"I've already thought of that," admitted Charlie. "It would be the worst thing I could do."

"What then?"

The idea was only half formed in Charlie's mind, but at least it indicated some intention.

"I think it's time that at last I saw Lucky Lu."

"I'm not sure that's strictly legal, now that he's issued writs."

It probably wasn't, thought Charlie. But being strictly legal had never been a consideration in the past.

"We don't have time to worry about legal niceties," said Charlie.

"Be careful then. Be bloody careful."

Charlie hesitated at the words.

"I will," he promised. Or dead, he thought.

It would have helped, decided Harvey Jones, had he had someone with whom he could have discussed the meeting. But the instructions had been explicit. So he had to reach a judgment by himself. The man was unusual, certainly. But was he any more than that? The apparent awareness of interrogation techniques was intriguing. But there were many sorts of people who might have experience of that. Lawyers, for instance. And insurance investigators would have had a lot of contact with the law. A smart lawyer would have spotted the inconsistency about the Chinese dockyard workers, too. Or again, someone who spent a lot of time involved with them.

Specially chosen to prove himself. That's what the Deputy Director had said.

And he didn't want to prove himself an idiot by suggesting British intelligence were some way interested, with a cover as good as his own.

He'd wait, he decided. Until he was sure. And only when he was convinced would he cable Langley and get them to run a check in London so that there could be some official instruction for them to work together. Ridiculous to operate separately, after all.

Jones smoothed the robe around him, looking across to where his suit hung crisp and fresh after its return from the hotel valet.

That was another thing he'd found difficult to accept about the man. For someone important enough to be investigating a £6,000,000 insurance claim, he was a scruffy son of a bitch.

Meant one thing, though. With a description like that, it wouldn't take the computer long to come up with the man's proper name. So they could even approach London with an identity, in case the bastards tried to deny their interest.

CHAPTER THIRTEEN

THE RECEPTION AREA was enormous and everywhere were pictures of L. W. Lu.

Charlie examined them with the professionalism of his teenage training, appreciating the care that had gone into their taking and selection. The biggest, a gigantic enlargement occupying nearly the whole wall behind the desk of identically uniformed girls, showed the millionaire with two American Presidents and another, only slightly smaller, with Henry Kissinger. Along another wall was a series showing Lu individually, and then in groups, with all the British Commonwealth leaders during the Singapore conference. And the area to the left was given over to a pictorial history of Lu's charity work, showing him at the two orphanages he had established for Vietnamese refugees after the fall of Saigon and touring wards of the hospitals which were maintained entirely by the charitable trust he had created.

"Christ," said Charlie mockingly, moving forward and looking for the lift he had been told would bypass the other eighteen floors of the skyscraper block from which Lu Industries were controlled and take him direct to the penthouse office.

He located it by the guards. Both were armed, he saw. A separate receptionist, male this time, sat behind them at a small desk.

"You have an appointment for eleven o'clock with Mr. Lu?" anticipated the man before Charlie could speak.

"Yes."

"We were told to expect you."

The lift door opened by some control, which the man obviously operated but which Charlie could not see, and as he entered he saw the man reach for a telephone to announce his arrival above. Predictably, there were more photographs lining the elevator panels, this time showing Lu at the launchings of his various tankers and passenger ships. The facing wall had pictures of the *Pride of America* leaving New York, another of its Hong Kong arrival, and a third showing Lu in a small boat alongside the destroyed hull. John Lu really did resemble his father, thought Charlie, studying the photographs. Except for the smile. The younger man was a miserable-looking sod. Charlie paused, considering the judgment. Not really miserable, he corrected. More apprehensive.

Despite the obvious entry he could have expected from the Willoughby company name and the warning from the increasingly distracted underwriter in a hurried telephone call earlier that morning that Lu's London office had made contact to establish he had directorial authority, Charlie had still been intrigued at the speed with which the millionaire had agreed to see him. He'd anticipated a delay of several days instead of the instantaneous agreement.

Another man, uniformed like his colleague on the ground floor, awaited Charlie when the elevator doors opened.

"Please," he said, inviting Charlie to follow.

This time the photographs around the walls were of world leaders. Charlie identified the nearest as President Giscard d'Estaing and former Prime Minister

Pierre Trudeau. And on easels this time because the wall area was entirely glass, giving a 180-degree view of Hong Kong, Kowloon, and the mainland beyond.

There were uniformed and armed guards in the corridor and even in three outer offices through which they had to pass to reach the door to Lu's personal office suite. It would be virtually impossible to make an unauthorised entry upon the man, realised Charlie, professionally.

Lu's office was very large, created from the corner of the building with the views of Kowloon and the New Territories. Rotating smoked-glass slats, running from floor to ceiling, gave the room an unexpectedly subdued lighting compared to the brightness of the other rooms through which he had passed. And there was a further surprise: here there were no photographs. A bookcase occupied one of the two unglassed walls, broken only by a doorway, and along the other were showcases containing models of boats.

Lu rose as Charlie entered, hurrying around his desk, hand outstretched, teeth glinting.

"Welcome, sir," he said, the hiss in his voice only just evident. "Welcome indeed."

For how long? wondered Charlie.

The millionaire personally led him to a couch away from the desk, then sat down in a matching easy chair.

"Some refreshment?"

"No thank you," refused Charlie.

"Nothing at all?"

"Nothing."

Charlie looked around the office again.

"What is it?" asked Lu.

"I was expecting your son to be present."

"John?"

"You appear to spend a lot of time together."

"No father could ask for a more dutiful son," he said.

"Isn't son-to-father loyalty a Chinese tradition?"

Lu paused.

"Filial attachments are important in Asia," he

agreed. "But unfortunately the ties appear to be becoming less important to the young of today."

"I've learned quite a lot of Chinese tradition since I've been here," said Charlie.

"You're not recently arrived?"

"No."

"Then I'm surprised."

"Surprised?"

"That you haven't called upon me sooner."

"I don't understand," said Charlie.

Lu made an expansive gesture.

"Surely this meeting means that there is to be no unpleasantness between your company and myself."

"Unpleasantness?"

"Over this business of the writs."

"I don't think I can promise that," said Charlie guardedly. The mechanical efficiency to which he'd so far been exposed probably meant that somewhere a tape recording was being made of the encounter. It was the sort of precaution he would have taken.

Momentarily Lu's smile dimmed.

"That's disappointing," he said.

"But inevitable, I'm afraid."

"You haven't come to agree settlement?"

"No."

Lu was forcing the discussion, realised Charlie. To get the response he wanted from the man, he needed time to seed some uncertainty.

"What then?" demanded the millionaire.

Shock him, decided Charlie.

"To warn you that under no circumstances will my company consider paying out one cent of the claims you have filed against us," he declared.

Lu settled back in the chair, shaking his head in apparent sadness. Not the reaction he had tried for, thought Charlie.

"Do you know," said Lu reflectively, "I really can't remember when anyone had the temerity to *warn* me about anything."

"I gather you lead a fairly protected life," said Charlie, gesturing to the outer doors.

Lu sighed, too obviously, at the intended sarcasm.

"So very unfortunate," he said, still maintaining the smile.

The sibilance was more noticeable, realised Charlie. So there was at least some slight annoyance. It wouldn't be enough.

"As unfortunate as the death of Robert Nelson?"

Lu nodded.

"I heard of the death of your man here," he said. "Such an able person . . . obtained more of my business than anyone else."

"Why, Mr. Lu?" said Charlie.

The smile was finally extinguished.

"Because I respected him and chose to give him the business."

"At 12 per cent, when the rest of the sealed bids quoted 10?"

For a moment the millionaire faltered.

"I can afford to give my business to whom I choose," he said.

"That's not business, Mr. Lu. That's charity. Or stupidity. Or an indication that you didn't expect the money to be out of your hands for very long. Just long enough for it to be the bait for which it was intended."

"I'm really not accustomed to rudeness," said Lu threateningly.

"I'm not being rude," said Charlie. "I'm asking a very pertinent question."

"After the sealed tenders had been taken up," said Lu, "we discovered that we were still uncovered to the extent of £6,000,000. Mr. Nelson's offer had not at that stage been accepted. Rather than reopen the other policies, which might have taken us, even further uninsured, dangerously near the sailing date from New York, I decided to give it to him. It was an oversight, really. It was all done at the very last moment."

"He told me about the rush," said Charlie. "And I think you are talking bullshit."

Lu winced at the crudeness. That hadn't worked either, thought Charlie.

"I'm not really concerned what you will accept or

not," said Lu. "I'm rich enough to do as I wish with my money."

"No one's that rich."

"I am. And I'll remind you that I'm used to being treated with proper respect because of it."

"And I'll remind you that I'm not being disrespectful," said Charlie. He was, he knew. Intentionally so. There had to be some way to penetrate the man's control.

"That's for me to decide," said Lu.

"There will be several things for you to decide today," agreed Charlie.

"Don't strain my patience," said Lu.

"Now you're issuing warnings," said Charlie.

"With far more ability to enforce them," said Lu.

"As it was enforced upon Robert Nelson?"

Lu sat impassively, hands cupped in his lap. It wasn't working, realised Charlie. Lu had sensed the manoeuvre and refused to react.

"I know that Nelson was murdered," announced Charlie. "And I know why."

Do *something*, for Christ's sake, he thought.

"All of which," said Lu, "would, I'm sure, be of great interest to the police. My only concern is in the settlement of my claim for the destruction of my ship, sorry as I am about Mr. Nelson's death."

"You destroyed your own ship," declared Charlie, "and had Robert Nelson killed when he tried to establish the reasons being spread by your people among the Chinese community."

Lu's smile came back, a patronising expression.

"I've made a mistake," he said. "I've admitted a madman to my office. And I'm usually so careful."

"As careful as you were in having the shipyard workers killed, knowing they could never withstand any cross-examination in court."

"More than one murder!" mocked Lu.

There had always been a desperation about the bluff, accepted Charlie. But he'd expected to unsettle the man far more than he had done. He should have resisted Lu's pace and prolonged the verbal fencing, he accepted. It was his own fault that he'd hurried the confrontation. More than hurried. Panicked it, in fact. Because of his nervousness of Harvey Jones. There had been a time when he wouldn't have made such a mistake, no matter what the pressure.

"You and, perhaps more important, your son have lost face once," persisted Charlie. "Try to press this claim in court and I'll ensure you'll be ridiculed not just in Asia but throughout the world. Are you prepared to risk that?"

"I haven't the remotest conception what you're talking about," said Lu, shaking his head.

"I will guarantee that in the English High Court my company will oppose your claim," said Charlie. "I'll see to it that every suspicion comes out. We'll label Robert Nelson's death for what it was. We'll demand to know in open court why you were prepared to pay 12 per cent on £6,000,000 and get a better answer than the one you've given me. We'll show the real reason . . . that your anti-communist campaign was always to be paid for by British insurance companies. . . ."

"Such nonsense," intruded Lu. "You're talking absolute nonsense."

". . . But we won't just stop there," carried on Charlie. "We'll ask questions about the gambling. And the brothelkeeping. And the heroin factories that supply America and Europe."

"Is there no crime for which I'm not to be held responsible?" sneered Lu. He infused the impression of boredom into his voice.

"I don't know of a man who used publicity more effectively than you," said Charlie, refusing Lu's jibe. "Are you prepared to risk the loss of face that such a court hearing would cause?"

Lu stood and for a moment Charlie thought he intended summoning the guards from the outer offices. Instead the man went to the desk, selected a cigar and returned to the chair, fumbling for the gold cutter on his watch chain.

"I congratulate you," announced Lu unexpectedly.

Charlie waited.

"It really was a most effective attempt," continued the millionaire. ". . . almost deserved to succeed."

"*Will* succeed," corrected Charlie, imagining a change of attitude at last.

"Oh no," said Lu. "I'm no longer treating you as a fool and neither must you regard me as one."

The attitude *had* changed, realised Charlie. But not as he had hoped.

"I've already told you," reminded Lu, "that I'm a very careful man. I begin nothing without the guarantee of success. . . ."

He stopped, waving a flame before his face. Charlie glanced towards the desk. He hadn't seen Lu turn off any recording device. But that's what the man had done, he accepted, under the guise of getting a cigar.

". . . I'm not arguing you wouldn't win judgment," said Charlie. "I'm saying it would be a court action that would destroy you and your reputation. . . ."

"And I asked you not to treat me like a fool," repeated Lu sadly. "We both of us know there will never be a court hearing."

"You'll withdraw the claim?"

Lu laughed at him, in genuine amusement.

"No," he said. "I won't withdraw the claim. I'll press it as hard as I am able. Because I know damned well that no lawyer, no matter how much filth or innuendo he hoped to smear, would risk fighting in court the case I am able to bring. . . ."

". . . I will . . ." tried Charlie, but Lu raised his hand imperiously, halting him.

". . . You need evidence," said Lu. "Better evidence than some doubt about a rich man's foible in paying more than he should for a policy he needed in a hurry. . . . You'll need witnesses, prepared to give evidence about a planned crime. And if you had that, it wouldn't be you sitting here. It would be the police. . . ."

Gently he tapped the ash from his cigar.

". . . Your lawyers might listen to your romanticising," said the millionaire. "They might even be curious. But they'd never introduce it into a court hearing.

Your company will settle. For the full amount. Because they have no option. My policy is legally incontestable. There's never been any risk of my being humiliated. Nor will there be. Ever."

He'd lost, accepted Charlie. Completely. Another thought came suddenly. Robert Nelson had died simply for attempting to establish the accusation at street level; he had actually challenged the man.

"You checked me with my London office before agreeing to meet me?" he said.

Lu nodded.

"I told you I leave nothing to chance."

"And they knew I was coming here today . . . to confront you with what I believed to be the truth?"

Lu's smiled broadened.

"You're giving me another warning," he anticipated.

"Were anything to happen to me, so soon after Robert Nelson's death and my visit here, the police might be forced into finding the proof that our lawyers might need to take the case to court."

It meant *admitting* defeat, recognised Charlie reluctantly. But that had been established anyway. Now he needed protection.

"Yes," agreed Lu. "They just might. I'll remember that."

At least, decided Charlie, rising and moving towards the door, he'd survived. From Lu anyway. But there was still Harvey Jones.

"You'll recommend your company to drop their resistance and settle?" said Lu expectantly.

Charlie stopped, turning.

"No," he said shortly.

"You can't win, you know."

"So people keep telling me."

"Perhaps you should listen to their advice."

"Perhaps."

"Don't become an irritant, will you?" demanded Lu.

Maybe he hadn't created as much safety as he had hoped, thought Charlie.

"Unfortunately," he said, at the door, "it seems to be a facility I have."

"Yes," said Lu, determined to master every exchange. "It could be unfortunate."

The millionaire was still sitting in the chair in which he had confronted Charlie when his son entered from the adjoining room.

"Well?" asked the older man.

"Kill him," insisted John Lu immediately.

"Fool," rejected Lu. "You spend so much time with the scum that you even think like them now."

"But he's got it; he's got it all."

The millionaire shook his head.

"He's got nothing. Not a shred of proof. And there's nowhere he can get it."

"What about the woman?"

"You chose badly there, didn't you?" demanded Lu, avoiding a direct answer.

The younger man, who had remained standing, shuffled awkwardly with the admission.

"She'd talk," he said.

"About what?" dismissed the millionaire.

"But she knows!"

"And everything we've got is concealed by companies layered upon companies and by nominees operating through other nominees," reminded Lu. "There is nothing directly linking us to anything. Who's going to start investigating us on the word of a whore?"

"She could still be a nuisance," said John in rare defiance.

"Oh, I think she should be punished," agreed Lu, as if correcting a misapprehension.

The son smiled.

"But properly this time," warned Lu.

"Of course."

Jenny Lin Lee would want to know of the arrangements for the funeral, Charlie decided. There was no reply throughout the afternoon to his repeated telephone calls, so after the inquest at which he gave evidence of identification and which returned the verdict which Superintendent Johnson had anticipated, he went to Robert Nelson's apartment.

The doorbell echoed back hollowly to him.

The caretaker was happy to open the door for fifty dollars and Charlie's assurance that he represented the dead man's company.

Already the rooms had a stale, unlived-in smell. Expertly he went from room to room, knowing why there had been no reply to the telephone. Nowhere was there a trace of the girl. Known in all the bars, she'd said. Which ones? he wondered.

As he turned to leave the apartment, his foot touched something, scuffing it along the carpet. Bending, he picked up a letter with a London postmark and the Willoughby company address embossed on the back, for return in case of non-delivery.

Aware of its contents, he opened it anyway, reading it in seconds. Sighing, he put into his pocket the underwriter's letter assuring Robert Nelson that he would not be personally affected or in any way harmed by the *Pride of America* fire.

"Not much," muttered Charlie savagely, closing the door.

CHAPTER FOURTEEN

SINCE THE ENCOUNTER with the American, Charlie had become overconscious of the feeling of being watched, making sudden and too obvious checks, so that had he been under surveillance any observer would have easily been able to avoid detection. Desperation. Like trying to bluff Lu. And this new idea. Further desperation, he recognised, forced upon him by the difference of the past to the present.

Before, the only consideration had been Charlie's Rules. Now it was Judge's Rules—the need not just to learn the truth and then act to his own satisfaction, but to that of barristers and law lords. It imposed a restriction to which he was unaccustomed—like trying to run with a shoelace undone. There seemed a very real possibility of falling flat on his face.

People spilled from the pavement into Des Voeux road, slowing the cars to a noisy, protesting crawl. Charlie used the movement of avoiding people to check around him, then abandoned the futile attempt, knowing that in such a throng any identification would be impossible.

He had expected the legation of the People's Republic of China to be an imposing building, perhaps even with a police guard. But so ordinary was it, slotted in among the shops and the cinema, that he was almost past before he realised he had found it.

He pushed slowly forward through the milling Chinese, smiling at the impression as he entered. Just like a betting shop. Even to the counters around the sides at which the people were filling in not their horse selections but their applications to return to mainland China.

He ignored the side benches, going straight to the reception desk. It was staffed by three men dressed in identical black-grey tunics.

"I wish to see Mr. Kuo," said Charlie. When the clerk did not react, Charlie added: "Mr. Kuo Yuan-ching."

"He knows you?"

"I telephoned. He said I was to call."

The man hesitated, then turned through a small door at the rear. Charlie moved to one side, to make room for the continual thrust of people. A hell of a lot of the five thousand seemed to regard it as a wasted swim and to be anxious to get back, he thought.

He was kept waiting for nearly fifteen minutes before the clerk returned and nodded his head towards the rear office. Charlie squeezed with difficulty past the counter and went into the room.

It was as spartan and functional as that through which he had just come. A desk, three filing cabinets, one upright chair for any visitors, the walls bare and unbroken by any official photographs, even of Mao Tse-tung.

"May I?" asked Charlie, hand on the chair back.

The man stared at him without any expression of greeting, then nodded. Like confronting a headmaster for the first time, thought Charlie. Christ, his feet hurt.

"You will take tea?" said the official.

It was a statement rather than an hospitable question.

"Thank you," said Charlie, accepting the ritual.

Kuo rang a handbell and from a side-door, almost immediately, appeared another tunicked man carrying a tray dominated by a large thermos. Around it were grouped teapot and cups.

"Proper Chinese tea," announced Kuo, pouring.

Charlie took the cup, sipping it.

"Excellent," he said politely. He had rushed almost everything else and made a balls of it, he thought. And this was his last chance, hopeless though the attempt might be, under the newly recognised rules. So the meeting could proceed at whatever pace the other man dictated.

Kuo topped up the pot from the thermos, then sat back, regarding Charlie again with a headmasterly look.

Charlie gazed back, vaguely disconcerted. Kuo was a square-bodied, heavily built man, dressed in the regulation tunic but with no obvious signs of his rank. Under its cap of thick black hair, the man's face was smooth and unlined.

Kuo nodded towards the telephone.

"You spoke of wanting help?"

"Yes," said Charlie.

"What?"

"I represent one of the consortium who insured the *Pride of America*. . . ."

". . . who now stand to lose a large sum of money."

"Who now stand to lose a large sum of money," agreed Charlie.

"And you don't want to pay?"

Can't pay, thought Charlie, sighing. There was something almost artificial at the communistic criticism of capitalism, he decided. As ritualistic as the tea drinking.

"We're trying to avoid paying out wrongly," he qualified. "And at the moment, we might be forced to."

"How is that?" demanded Kuo.

"The liner was not set alight be agents of the People's Republic of China," declared Charlie.

For the first time there was reaction from the

man—no facial expression but an uncertain hesitation before he spoke again.

"If it is an assurance of that which you want, then of course you have it," said Kuo. "The accusation has been ridiculous from the start."

For someone of Kuo's control, it had been a clumsy response, thought Charlie.

"I want more than assurance," he said.

"What?"

"Proof."

Kuo leaned forward over the desk, pouring more tea.

"How long have you been in Hong Kong?" he asked, settling back into his chair.

"Little over a week," said Charlie.

"Then you must have seen the police?"

"Yes."

"And Mr. Lu?"

"Yes."

"So we must be almost at the bottom of the list," decided Kuo.

Charlie considered his reply. Was Kuo seeking an apology, imagining some insult in the order of priority? There seemed no point in evading the accusation.

"Yes," he admitted. "At the bottom."

Kuo smiled—a brief, unexpected expression.

"You're very honest," he said.

"If I thought I'd achieve more by lying, then I would," said Charlie.

Again the smile flickered into place.

"Very honest indeed."

Charlie sipped his tea. Again he'd made the proper response, he realised, relieved.

"Even if you are prepared to help me," Charlie went on, in explanation, "it might not be possible for you to do so."

"Why?"

"I believe Lu destroyed his own ship," said Charlie. "I believe that he used gambling debts to force the shipyard workers into doing it and then had them murdered by someone else who had got into debt like the first two. . . ."

Charlie hesitated. Kuo remained impassive on the other side of the desk.

"Believe," repeated Charlie. "But cannot prove to the satisfaction that would be demanded by an English court in which Lu is sueing for payment. But there might be a way to obtain that proof. . . ."

". . . by seeing if a prison cook named Fan Yung-ching has returned to his family in Hunan?"

Charlie nodded, letting the curiosity reach his face.

"We are not entirely ignorant of the affair," said Kuo.

"Then help me prove the truth of it," urged Charlie. "The real truth."

"You expect my country to help a capitalist institution save a fortune!"

"I expect China to have the proper awareness of the harm that could be caused to its relations with Washington if this remains unchallenged," said Charlie.

"An insurance official with a politician's argument," mused Kuo.

"A logical, sensible argument," corrected Charlie. He sounded as pompous as Johnson, he thought.

"Come now," said Kuo. "Lu has the irritation of a droning insect on a summer's day. Are you seriously suggesting an impediment between my country and America from someone as insignificant?"

"The *Pride of America* was built with an enormous grant from the American Government. And then sustained by an equally enormous grant, until it became blatantly uneconomical. Millions of dollars of American taxpayers' money supported that ship. And there was a *pride* in it. The destruction, within weeks of leaving America, is far from insignificant. And I'm sure there are people within your Foreign Ministry who feel the same way. . . ."

Charlie paused, tellingly.

". . . and if you didn't think so, too," he said, "you wouldn't be as familiar with the details as you obviously are."

Again there was the brief, firefly smile.

"Not only honest," said the Chinese. "But remarkably perceptive as well."

"Am I wrong?"

Kuo fingered his teacup, finally looking up.

"No," he admitted, matching Charlie's earlier honesty. "You're not wrong."

"Then help me," said Charlie again.

"How?"

"If the cook has returned to Hunan . . ." began Charlie.

". . . He has," cut off Kuo.

Charlie felt the sweep of familiar excitement at the awareness that he could win. Lu's boastful word, he remembered. But that's all it was, a boast. In himself, Charlie knew, the need was far deeper. Sir Archibald had recognised it; one of the few who had. And used it quite calculatingly. But openly, of course. "Go out and win, Charlie." Always the same encouragement. And so he'd gone out and won. Because he'd had to. Just as he'd had to win, provably and demonstrably so, when he'd realised Sir Archibald's successors were trying to beat him. And then again when they'd begun the chase. "Go out and win, Charlie." No matter who gets hurt. Or dies. Poor Edith.

Charlie began concentrating, considering another thought. He'd expected the Chinese to be properly concerned, but to have established already the return to China of the Hunan cook showed a determined investigation.

"Superintendent Johnson told me he had sought assistance from you," said Charlie.

"He wants the man returned to the colony."

"And that's not possible?" probed Charlie gently.

"It might not be thought wise."

"I wouldn't need his return to fight Lu in the English High Court," assured Charlie.

"How then?"

"Give me an entry visa to China," said Charlie. "Let me interview the man, in the presence of your officials and someone from the British embassy in Peking who can notarise the statement as being properly made and, therefore, legally admissible in an English court."

He'd been involved in British espionage for two decades, reflected Charlie. And in that time used a dozen overseas embassies. There could easily be an earlier encountered diplomat now assigned to Peking who might recognise him. He would, thought Charlie, spend the rest of his life fleeing through a hall of distorted mirrors and shying away from half-seen images of fear.

Kuo indicated the teapot, but Charlie shook his head. The man added to his own cup, apparently considering the request.

"You must tell me one thing," he said.

"What?"

"If we make this facility available to you . . . if he makes a full confession about what happened, can you absolutely guarantee Lu's claim being publicly discussed in an open court so that the man will be exposed for the fraud he is?"

Now Charlie remained unspeaking, balancing the demand. It was impossible to anticipate the statement. Or its admissibility in court, despite the attempted legality of having a British embassy official present. It would be sufficient to beat Lu. But more probably in private negotiations with lawyers than in an open court challenge.

"It would mean Lu's claim against my company would fail," predicted Charlie.

"But not that the man would have to be confronted in a court for everyone to witness?"

"I cannot guarantee that."

"I respect you again for your frankness," said the legation head.

"You knew that, without my telling you," said Charlie.

"Yes," said Kuo. "I knew it."

Charlie controlled the almost imperceptible sigh. Another test passed, he decided.

"I would try to ensure that my company made a public announcement of any withdrawal by Lu," promised Charlie. "And that, by its very inference, would show the claim to be false."

"But isn't it sometimes a condition of out-of-court settlements that there should be no publicity?"

"There appears little you haven't considered," said Charlie.

"No," agreed Kuo. "There isn't."

"Does that mean you can give me an immediate decision about a visa?"

Kuo shook his head at the eagerness.

"Oh no," he said. "I have to refer to Peking."

"So there could be a delay."

"There normally is."

"But this isn't a normal case," reminded Charlie.

"No."

"So when would you expect to get a decision?"

"What would you say if I asked you to return this time tomorrow?"

"I would say that you seem to have been expecting me."

Kuo laughed, his face fully relaxing for the first time.

"We were," he said. "In fact, I'm surprised it's taken you so long."

The wind began to freshen in sudden, breathy gusts as it always does before the sudden summer downpours in Hong Kong, and the priest started to hurry, frowning above his prayer book at the clouds bubbling over the Peak. Why shouldn't he? thought Charlie. Despite a congregation of only one, the man had persisted with a full service, even the fifteen-minute promise of the glory awaiting Robert Nelson compared to the unhappiness of the life he had known. So why should he get wet? From the left the gravediggers hovered, shovels in hand, as anxious as the priest that the grave should not become water-logged.

Charlie shook his head, refusing the invitation to cast the first sod down upon the coffin.

The priest smiled slightly, happy at the saved minute.

". . . and so," he intoned, "I commit the body of Robert Nelson to the earth and his soul to Heaven. . . ."

He turned expectantly to Charlie, who was unsure what to do. Finally he backed away, realising it was over. The priest fell into step beside him.

"Surprised at the turn-out," he said genially.

"Yes," agreed Charlie. He'd worked methodically through the bars of the Wanchai and then Kowloon, trying to locate Jenny Lin Lee. And got shrugs and blank faces and assurances that she was unknown.

"Particularly from someone so respected in the community."

Charlie looked sideways. The priest smiled back ingenuously. The man didn't know, decided Charlie. But then, how could he?

"Perhaps they were busy," dismissed Charlie.

The priest frowned.

"That's not usually an obstruction among the European community here," he said defensively.

"At least he'll never know how little they cared," said Charlie, jerking his head back in the direction of the grave.

The priest stopped on the narrow pathway, face creased in distaste.

"That's hardly respectful of the dead," he complained.

"Neither is a business community ignoring the funeral of a man who's worked here all his life," snapped Charlie. Wasn't there ever a circumstance when he would not have to weigh and consider his words? he thought wearily.

"Quite," retreated the priest immediately. "Very sad."

The pathway split, one way going back to the church, the other to the lychgate exit. The first rain splattered the stones as they paused, to part.

"Good-bye," said the priest, grateful to have escaped getting wet.

"Thank you," said Charlie.

He was almost at the covered gateway before he saw Harvey Jones. He stopped, careless of the downpour.

"I startled you," apologised the American.

"Yes," said Charlie.

"I'm sorry."

Charlie said nothing. He should have seen the man, he thought. Been aware of his presence at least. Perhaps his instinct *was* failing.

"Hadn't you better get under cover?" said Jones. "You're getting soaked."

Charlie pressed under the tiny roof, turning back to look over the churchyard to avoid the American's direct attention. The gravediggers were scrabbling the earth into the grave, careless how they filled it. The poor bugger even got buried messily.

"Arrived too late to join the service," said Jones, still apologising.

"You'd have been lost in the crowd," said Charlie sarcastically. "Why did you come?"

"Wanted to see you."

"Why?"

Because the man's curiosity was increasing rather than diminishing, thought Charlie, answering his own question.

"See how you're getting on," said Jones.

Liar, thought Charlie.

"You'd have kept drier waiting at the hotel."

"Nothing else to do," said the American easily. "Perhaps it was the rain that kept everyone away."

"He wasn't very popular," said Charlie.

"Certainly not with someone."

Charlie ignored the invitation.

"How's the investigation going?" asked Jones, forced into the direct demand.

"Nowhere."

"Pity."

"Yes."

"Didn't suggest a separate autopsy?"

"What?" said Charlie, forgetting.

"Separate autopsy," repeated Jones. "Try to find something upon which Johnson could have worked."

"Decided it would be a waste of time."

"So what *have* you done?"

Spent all my time trying to avoid you, thought Charlie.

"Poked about," he said.

"And found what?"

"Nothing. What about you?"

"Nothing."

It was as if his anxiety were forcing the breath from him, making it impossible for him to create proper sentences. It would not be difficult for Jones to discern the attitude. And for his curiosity to increase. The rain began lessening. Soon he would be able to escape.

"Still might be better if we worked together," said Jones.

"I prefer to stay on my own," rejected Charlie

"Wonder what the Chinese think about it?" said Jones suddenly.

Charlie made an unknowing gesture.

"Why not ask them?"

"Might well do that," accepted the American. "Do they have representation here?"

"I believe so," said Charlie, playing the game. So Jones had been out there somewhere in the crowd and seen him enter the legation. And wanted him to know. Why? An offer to identify himself, like wearing a school tie?

"Yes indeed, I might well do that," repeated the American.

"Let me know how you get on," said Charlie.

"Of course," promised Jones. *"I'll* keep my side of the bargain."

Another invitation, Charlie recognised.

"It's stopped raining," he said, nodding beyond the lychgate.

"Can I give you a lift?"

"I've got a taxi waiting," said Charlie.

"I'll let you know what Kuo Yuan-ching says," undertook Jones, as he walked from the churchyard.

"Who?" said Charlie, avoiding the trap.

"Kuo Yuan-ching," said the American again. "I gather he's the man to see."

Charlie stretched back against the seat as his car started its switchback descent towards the Central district. The tension made him physically ache, he realised. And tired. He blinked his eyes open, reflecting upon his encouter with Harvey Jones. And because he was tired, he was making mistakes. There had been no reason why he shouldn't have told the American of his visit to the Chinese official. All he had done was risk being found out in a lie and possibly arousing the man's suspicions further. And there were more than enough as it was.

"You're not thinking fast enough, Charlie," he told himself.

"So he's behaved exactly as you predicted?" said the inner council chairman.

"Yes," said Chiu. Modestly, he kept the satisfaction from his voice.

"You will deal with him personally?"

"I think it's best."

"And ensure every preparation is made?"

"Yes."

"I wonder how clever this Englishman is?"

"It doesn't really matter now, does it?" said Chiu, allowing the conceit.

"I suppose not," agreed the chairman.

CHAPTER FIFTEEN

CHARLIE got off the train at Sheung Shui and looked towards the Shum Chun River that formed the border. Almost as far as the Lo Wu bridge there was a confused crush of people. He began to walk towards the crossing but had almost immediately to step aside for a herd of pigs being driven into the New Territories and in the direction of Hong Kong.

Impossible to control, remembered Charlie. That's what Johnson had said. Difficult even to decide which way most of them were going.

There was no logical reason for any challenge, but Charlie still felt the involuntary stomach tightening when he offered his passport at the British end of the control. The official glanced at him briefly, compared the picture, checked the visa, and waved him on. Would he ever lose the apprehension? he wondered, walking onto the bridge towards China. Better if he didn't. Frightened, he reacted quicker.

At the Chinese check, he offered not just his passport but the letter which Kuo Yuan-ching had given him earlier that day. Immediately there was a smile of expectation, and at a gesture from the official, another Chinese walked forward from a small room behind the passport booth.

"My name is Chiu Chin-mao," introduced the second man. "I am to be your escort to Peking."

He retrieved Charlie's passport, waving to indicate that he should bypass the queue that stretched before him. Obediently the people parted and Chiu stretched out to take Charlie's overnight shoulder grip and briefcase.

Feeling vaguely embarrassed at the special treatment, Charlie surrendered the bags and fell into step with the other man.

"We expected you earlier," said Chiu. Like the men in the Hong Kong legation, he wore the regulation grey-black tunic. He was a thin, bespectacled man, with an intense way of examining people when he spoke, as if suspecting the responses they made.

"I didn't anticipate the people," admitted Charlie. He nodded towards another herd of pigs. "Or the livestock."

"Trade is extensive in this part of China," said Chiu watchfully.

The treaty guaranteeing British sovereignty was not accepted by Peking, remembered Charlie.

"Of course," he said, wanting to avoid a political polemic.

The official seemed disappointed.

Once free of the immediate border, it was easier to move, despite the bicycles. They appeared to be everywhere, cluttering the kerb edges and thronging the oddly traffic-free roads.

Seeing Charlie's look, Chiu said: "To cycle is to remain fit."

"Yes," said Charlie. If he let the man get it out of his system, perhaps he'd stop.

"We have a long way to go," said Chiu, looking at his watch.

"I know."

"But we can still make our connections," added the

Chinese. "We will go by train to Canton and from there fly to Peking."

"I appreciate very much the trouble you have taken," said Charlie.

"My ministry regards your visit as important," said Chiu.

"Ministry?"

"I am attached to the political section of the Foreign Ministry," elaborated the man.

Different from normal, recognised Charlie. They really were going to enormous trouble.

At the station they appeared to be expected, bypassing the normal barriers with an attentive escort of railway officials.

The train seemed almost as crowded as the border bridge, but Chiu went confidently ahead of the railwaymen until he found the empty carriage he was apparently seeking and stood back for Charlie to enter.

"Reserved," he announced.

So much for equality for all, thought Charlie. He sat back as Chiu dismissed the officials in a tumble of Chinese, staring through the window at the last-minute rush before departure. For the first time in almost a fortnight, he thought, he did not have the impression of being watched. It was a tangible relief.

He turned to the man opposite.

"I am still surprised that my visa approval was so prompt," he said, sweeping his hand out to encompass the carriage. "And at all this assistance."

"I have already said your visit is regarded as important," reminded Chiu.

"Less than a day is still fast," insisted Charlie.

"Not for China," said Chiu, seeing the opportunity.

The train lurched, shuddering forward clear of the station. Like most rail systems upon which he had travelled throughout the world, it appeared to go through every back garden. But unlike the other systems, there was a difference. Here each garden was immaculate and cared for, like entries in a horticultural exhibition. Which was the purpose, decided Charlie. But a public relations exhibition, not a horticultural one.

Once in the open country, they travelled along the spine of high embankments. On either side, in the regimented paddy fields, peasants crouched knee-deep in the irrigation water beneath the shade of their lampshade hats.

"You will be staying in the Hsin Chiao hotel, in what was once the Legation district of Peking," announced Chiu.

The only hotel in the city with a bar, remembered Charlie. He wondered if he'd have anything to celebrate.

Anticipating another didactic as Chiu moved to speak, Charlie said quickly: "It is surprising that you've allowed me access to this man in preference to the Hong Kong police."

"The police would demand his return," said Chiu, as if that were explanation enough.

"But that would surely achieve the same effect as letting me obtain a statement . . . better, even. It would guarantee a court hearing."

Chiu looked across at him tolerantly.

"It would also establish a precedent," he said.

They were interrupted by the carriage door opening. Charlie turned to see a file of white-coated men.

"I've arranged for lunch to be served here in the compartment," explained Chiu.

Neither spoke while the table was erected between them and the dishes laid out.

"There are knives and forks, if you wish," said Chiu solicitously.

"Chopsticks will be fine," said Charlie. There appeared no courtesy the Chinese authorities had overlooked.

As they started to eat, Charlie said: "So the man will go unpunished?"

Chiu paused, chopsticks before his face.

"Oh no," he insisted quietly. "People who bring disgrace to China never go unpunished."

The special treatment continued when they reached Canton. A car was at the station to take them directly to the airport. There they again skirted all the formalities, driving past the departure building to the waiting aircraft. Predictably, their seats were reserved.

"The man is being brought from Hunan, to enable your meeting to take place in the capital," announced Chiu, as they belted themselves in for take-off.

"That's very helpful," said Charlie.

"We thought it better."

"The British embassy . . ." started Charlie.

". . . Ambassador Collins has promised an official to notarise any meeting," finished Chiu, enjoying the constant indications of their efficiency. "My Ministry has already approached them."

"Collins?"

A movement went through Charlie, as if he were physically cold. Not the same man, he thought, wildly. It couldn't be. Just a coincidence, that's all. He smothered the hope objectively. Now he was thinking like Willoughby. Unrealistically. And he'd already done too much of that.

Could still be a coincidence, he decided. Not a particularly unusual name, after all. Then again, it might not be. About due for ambassadorial promotion when they'd met. The First Secretary at the Prague embassy, remembered Charlie. Prissy man, resenting the London instruction to provide whatever help Charlie might demand. The department were giving him that sort of authority then, still believing the defection to be the biggest intelligence coup of the decade. The visit to Czechoslovakia had been to arrange the final details of the crossing.

"You know him?" asked the Chinese.

"No," said Charlie. I hope, he thought. There'd even been an argument between them.

Chiu stared at him curiously.

Just when everything had at last seemed to be going so easily, thought Charlie. Why hadn't he checked at the High Commission in Hong Kong? Taken one telephone call, that's all. He'd even anticipated the danger, in Kuo's office. Careless again; unthinking.

The aircraft doors thumped closed and the No Smoking and seatbelts signs flicked on. There was nothing he could do, realised Charlie. Not a bloody thing.

"My Ministry have taken a very unusual decision in admitting you," said Chiu. "We hope it will work out satisfactorily."

"So do I," said Charlie sincerely. In so many ways, he thought. He'd certainly need the hotel bar. But not for a celebration.

Harvey Jones leaned against the rail of the ferry taking him from Hong Kong to Kowloon, gazing down into the churned waters of the harbour. Far away the *Pride of America* looked like one of those beached whales that sometimes came ashore along the Miami coastline, driven to suicide by sea parasites infecting their skins. His parents had sent him pictures in their last letter from Fort Lauderdale, the one in which they'd assured him how happily they were settling down into retirement.

Pity he couldn't send them a postcard. Be bad security, he knew. Perhaps he'd visit them, when he got back. He might even have something about which to boast. Then again, he might not.

Jones drove his fist in tiny, impatient movements against the rail. Why, he wondered, were the damned Chinese being so helpful to the bloody man? And they *were* being helpful. Openly so. He hadn't even had to make it obvious that he'd followed the man to the legation offices. Kuo had freely admitted it. Almost volunteered it.

"... *special chance* ... *to prove yourself*...."

He was being beaten, decided Jones. By a tied-in-the-middle-with-string hayseed of an agent who should have been put out to pasture long ago. And he *was* an agent, no matter how closely he tried to hide behind the insurance-investigator crap. Jones was sure of it.

The American stared up, irritated by another realisation. To ask Washington to pressure London for co-operation now would be an open admission of failure. Best to wait. At least until the man came back. It would be easy to gauge whether the visit had been worthwhile. That was it. Just wait and trick the bastard into some sort of admission. Then put the arm on him.

The ferry nudged against the dock and Jones got into line to disembark.

Still failure, though. Whether he did it now or later.

It wasn't going as he had hoped, he admitted to himself reluctantly. In fact, it was turning out to be a complete fuck up.

Jones had cleared the quayside by the time Jenny Lin Lee finally left the same ferry. For a moment she stared across towards Hong Kong island, then started towards Kowloon.

Already they would know she had arrived. Been warned to expect her, in fact. Just as the hotels and then the bars in the Wanchai had been warned to refuse her, forcing her lower and lower.

She turned right, along the Salisbury Road and in front of the Peninsula Hotel which Jones had just entered, and on towards the harbour slums.

That's where the Mao Tai shacks and the short-time houses were. All she could expect now. Or would be allowed. No Europeans, of course. Or even clean Chinese. Just the blank-eyed, diseased men of the fishing junks and the shipyards.

She could avoid the pain, she knew, feeling for the assurance of the hypodermic in her shoulder bag. There would be no difficulty in obtaining it, not until she'd really established a dependence. Then it might be difficult. Impossible, eventually. But that hadn't happened yet. Weeks away. And she had to take away the feeling.

CHAPTER SIXTEEN

FAN YUNG-CHING, the former prison cook, was a wizened, dried-out old man, tissue-paper skin stretched over the bones of his face and hands, making him almost doll-like. A very ugly doll, thought Charlie.

The man crouched rather than sat on the other side of the interview bench, skeletal hands across his stomach as if he were in physical pain. Which he probably was. Fear leaked from him, souring the room with his smell. Soon, decided Charlie, the man would wet himself. Charlie had been in many rooms, confronting many men as frightened as this. Always, at some stage, their bladder went. He hoped that was the only collapse. Often it wasn't.

It was a small, box-shaped chamber, crowded because of the number of people who had to be present.

The interpreter who would translate Charlie's questions was immediately to his left, arms upon the table, waiting with a notepad before him. Behind, at a narrow bench, sat Chiu Chin-mao. With him was the official from the legal section of the British embassy.

Geoffrey Hodgson, the man had introduced himself.

Typical diplomat-lawyer posted because of an ability with languages.

Charlie looked at the lawyer and Hodgson smiled hopefully, just as he'd smiled confirming in unwitting conversation the ambassador's former posting to Prague.

"Expects you at the embassy after the interview," Hodgson had said.

No escape then.

It would have been four years, Charlie had calculated. And not more than three hours together. The man would have encountered thousands of people in that time. And not known about the outcome of Charlie's visit to Czechoslovakia anyway, because of the embarrassment to the department of what had actually happened.

Scarce reason to remember him. Wrong to panic then. Pointless anyway. At least he knew in advance. It gave him an advantage: too slight.

Charlie continued his examination of the room. At a third table sat two bilingual notetakers, tape-recording machines between them.

As efficiently organised as everything else, decided Charlie.

"Shall we start?" he said.

"There should be an oath, if the man has a religion," warned Hodgson.

Fan shook his head to the interpreter's question.

"An affirmation, at least," insisted Hodgson. It was an unusual situation and he didn't want any mistakes.

"He understands," said the interpreter.

The man paused as one of the notetakers made an adjustment to the recorder, then quoted the undertaking to the old man. Haltingly, eyes locked on to the table in front of him, Fan repeated his promise that the statement would be the truth. He was wiping one hand over the other in tiny washing movements. He was too frightened to lie, Charlie knew.

The affirmation over, Fan hurriedly talked on, bobbing his hand in fawning, pleading motions.

"He begs forgiveness," said the interpreter. "He says

he was forced to do what he did . . . that he did not know it was a poison he was introducing into the men's food. He was told that it was a substance merely to make them ill, to cause a delay to the trial. . . ."

It was going to be more disjointed than he had expected, realised Charlie. He turned to Hodgson.

"Would there be any difficulty about admissibility if the transcript is shown to be a series of questions and answers?"

The British lawyer pursed his lips doubtfully.

"Shouldn't be," he said. "Providing that it couldn't be argued that the questions were too leading . . . you must not suggest the answers you want."

Charlie turned back to the cook.

"Does he know the man who gave him the substance?"

"The same man who threatened me," replied Fan, through the interpreter.

"What is his name?"

"Johnny Lu."

Charlie reached into his briefcase, bringing out one of the many photographs of the millionaire's son it had been automatic for him to bring. It had been taken at the press conference just after the liner had sailed from New York and showed the man next to his father.

"This man?" he asked.

Fan squinted at the picture, myopically.

"Yes," he said finally.

Charlie looked towards the recorders.

"Let the transcript show he has identified a picture of John Lu taken aboard the *Pride of America*," he dictated formally.

The proof, Charlie thought. The proof that Johnson had demanded. And which would save Willoughby. What, he wondered, would save him?

"Why did he threaten you?" he said, coming back to the old man.

". . . I owed money . . . money I had lost at Mah jong. I did not have it. . . ."

"What was the threat?"

"That he would have me hurt . . . badly hurt."

"Tell me what he said."

". . . that if I put what he gave me into their food, he would not let me be hurt . . . that it would cancel my debt."

"Were you at any time told what to do by anyone representing the government of China?"

Fan looked hurriedly to the interpreter and then across at Chiu, to whom the other Chinese in the room had been constantly deferent.

He shook his head.

"You must reply," insisted Charlie.

"No," said Fan.

"What about the men who died . . . those accused of causing the fire . . . ?"

It was a remote chance but worth trying.

"I do not know," said Fan.

"Did they gamble?" pressed Charlie.

Fan nodded. "Sometimes with me."

"Be careful," interrupted Hodgson from the side. "If just one section is challenged, it could have the effect of casting doubt on the whole statement."

"Did they win or lose?" Charlie asked the Chinese, nodding his acceptance of the lawyer's warning.

"Sometimes win. Sometimes lose," said Fan unhelpfully.

"Did John Lu cancel your debt?"

"He told me to go to him to get a paper. But I did not."

"Why?"

"I was frightened I would get killed. I ran away."

Fan gave an involuntary shudder and a different smell permeated the room. He'd been right, realised Charlie. It always happened.

"What did John Lu say would happen to the men who had caused the fire?"

"Just that they would become ill . . . nothing more."

"Why did he want that?"

"He said it would get into the newspapers . . . that it was important."

"Why?"

"I do not know."

He wanted nothing more from the man, Charlie knew. It had seemed ridiculously easy. But the rest of the day wasn't going to be.

He sat back, looking to Chiu.

"Thank you," he said.

"That is all?"

The Foreign Ministry official appeared surprised.

"It is enough," assured Charlie.

"There has been much trouble taken," said Chiu. "A mistake would be unfortunate."

"To go on might create just such a mistake," said Charlie, looking to Hodgson for support.

The lawyer nodded agreement.

"You came pretty close on one or two occasions as it was," he said.

"How long will it take to notarise this statement?" asked Charlie.

"Fifteen minutes," said Hodgson. "Won't take much longer to prepare it, either, I wouldn't think."

Charlie came back to Chiu.

"So I could return to Hong Kong first thing tomorrow?" he said. He had to limit his stay in Peking to the minimum, he had decided. Even if he identified him, Collins would have no reason to attempt his detention. The risk was in querying his presence with London. And by the time that was answered, he could be clear of Hong Kong. Running again.

Chiu was still unhappy with the brevity of the account, Charlie knew.

"If you wish," said the Chinese stiffly.

He did wish, thought Charlie. It wasn't just the new danger of the ambassador. He shouldn't forget the curiosity of Harvey Jones. At least he could escape that now. One problem replaced by another.

Charlie turned to the trembling figure sitting opposite. Fan still gazed steadfastly down at the table, not realising the questioning was over.

People who bring disgrace to China never go unpunished, Chiu had said. Hardly surprising the poor bastard had pissed himself.

"Will you tell him I am grateful," Charlie said to the interpreter. "He has been of great assistance."

Fan stared up at the translation. Even he was bewildered that it was over so quickly.

Charlie rose, ending the interview.

"Right," said Hodgson briskly. "Let's get along to the embassy, shall we?"

First, thought Charlie, he'd need a toilet.

"Quite the most unusual city to which I've ever been," volunteered the lawyer in the car taking them to the embassy.

"Yes," said Charlie. It didn't appear to have a centre, he thought. Rather it was sprawl upon sprawl of squares.

"Do you know that underneath all the buildings and offices there are nuclear shelters?" said Hodgson.

"No."

"It's a fact," insisted the lawyer. "The Chinese are paranoiac about an attack from Russia. They reckon they can clear the entire city in fifteen minutes."

That's what he needed, mused Charlie. A bombproof hole in the ground to which he could run at the first sign of danger.

"We've arrived," announced Hodgson.

To what? wondered Charlie. Despite his preparedness, he still faltered at the entrance to the ambassador's study, knowing as he did so that the reaction would look strange but momentarily unable to control the urge to turn and run.

"Come in, come in," encouraged the ambassador. "Not often we get visitors from home. And under such strange circumstances."

Collins had altered very little, Charlie decided. Not physically, anyway. He continued into the room, taking the outstretched hand. The man's face remained blank. Please God let it stay that way, prayed Charlie.

"Sherry," fussed Collins, indicating the decanter.

"Thank you," accepted Charlie. Not more than three hours, he thought again. How good was the man's memory?

"Astonishing business, this fire," said Collins, offering Charlie the glass.

"Very."

The man's manner had changed since their last meeting, even if his appearance had not. He was more polished than he had been in Prague; showed more confidence. But it would only be surface change, guessed Charlie. Still be a prissy sod.

"The Chinese chap made a full confession, did he?"

"Full enough," said Charlie. "It will be enough for us to challenge Lu's claim in the High Court."

"Have to make a report to London about it," said the ambassador, as if the idea had just occurred to him.

"Of course," said Charlie uneasily. "I understand the Hong Kong police have asked officially for assistance."

Collins nodded.

"No reply yet to my Note," he said.

He suddenly put his head to one side.

"Have we met before?" he demanded.

Charlie brought the sherry glass to his lips, knowing an immediate reply would have been impossible for him.

"Met before?" he echoed dismissively. "I don't think so. Not often I take sherry with a British ambassador."

No strain in his voice, he recognised gratefully. Sweat was flooding his back, smearing his shirt to him.

Collins laughed politely.

"Odd feeling there's been another occasion," he insisted.

"There must be so many people," said Charlie.

"Quite," agreed Collins.

"Do you anticipate the authorities will send the cook back?" said Charlie, trying to move the man on.

"They helped you," pointed out the diplomat.

"But only to obtain a statement. I gather they feel to turn the man over to the Hong Kong police would be establishing a precedent for any future cases. And they are unwilling to make such a sweeping commitment."

"Quite," said Collins again.

The ambassador was still examining him curiously.

"And as far as they are concerned, a High Court challenge will be as good as any criminal court proceedings," said Charlie.

"Ever been to Lagos?" blurted Collins, snapping his fingers in imagined recollection.

"Never," said Charlie. The perspiration would be visible on his face, he knew. And the room was really quite cold.

Collins moved his head doubtfully at the rejection.

"Usually got a good eye for faces," he apologised.

"I'd have remembered," said Charlie.

"Quite," said Collins.

Since their last meeting, the man had affected an air of studied vagueness, recognised Charlie. The attitude irritated him.

"How long you staying in Peking?"

"I've got what I came for," said Charlie. "I'm leaving as early as possible tomorrow morning."

"Oh," said Collins, in apparent disappointment. "Going to invite you to dinner tomorrow evening. Like I said, not often we get visitors from home."

"Very kind," refused Charlie. "But we've got to file an answer in the London courts as soon as possible."

"Quite."

Just a stupid mannerism? wondered Charlie. Or the thoughtless use of a favourite word, to feign interest while he tried to recall their other meeting.

"Stockholm?" tried Collins, gesturing with his finger.

Charlie shook his head.

"Never been there," he said. The man would persist, Charlie knew. He looked the sort of person who played postal chess and did crossword puzzles, enjoying little challenges.

Charlie looked obviously at his watch.

"I've a four o'clock appointment at the Foreign Ministry with Mr. Chiu," he improvised. He didn't and there was a danger of the ambassador discovering the lie. But it was the best escape he could manage. And there was an even greater danger in continuing this conversation.

"I'll check with Hodgson," said Collins, taking the hint.

He spoke briefly into the internal telephone, smiling over at Charlie as he replaced the receiver.

"All done," he said.

Almost immediately there was a movement from behind and the lawyer entered at the ambassador's call, carrying a file of documents.

"The Chinese original," he itemised. "And a British translation. Both notarised by me and witnessed by the First Secretary. I've also annotated the identified photograph and sworn a statement that it was this one seen by the man."

"You've been very kind," said Charlie, including the ambassador in the thanks.

"That's what we're here for," said Collins, rising with Charlie.

The ambassador walked with him to the study door. Charlie was aware of his attention.

"Amazing," said the ambassador, when they reached the hallway. "Just can't lose the feeling that I know you from somewhere."

"Thank you again," avoided Charlie.

"Sure about tomorrow night?"

"Quite sure. I'm sorry."

Charlie hesitated immediately outside the embassy buildings. He was trembling, he realised. Almost noticeably so. He straightened his arms against his sides, trying to control the emotion. After his discovery at Sir Archibald's vault, when he had realised they were chasing him, there had been times when he had felt helplessly trapped in a contracting room, with the walls and ceiling slowly closing in upon him. It had been a frightening, claustrophobic sensation. And a long time since he had encountered it. But it was very strong now.

"Well?" demanded Clarissa Willoughby.

"I'll have to make the statement soon," admitted the underwriter.

"Even before you finally hear from Hong Kong?"

"It's a criminal offence knowingly to go on trading without funds to meet your obligations," said Willoughby.

"Criminal!"

"Yes."

"Christ, I couldn't stand you appearing in court, as well."

"I didn't think you intended to stand anything."

"I don't," said the woman positively.

"Where are you going?"

"I haven't made up my mind. Does it matter?"

"I suppose not."

"I feel very sorry for you, Rupert. I really do."

She spoke in the manner of a person discovering that a friend's pet was having to be put down, thought the underwriter.

"Thank you. When do you intend to leave?"

"End of the week, I suppose," said the woman.

She smiled.

"You really are being remarkably civilised," she said.

"Isn't that what we've always been?" he said, the bitterness showing for the first time. "Remarkably civilised."

"If it confirms Lu's involvement with the fire, then surely it's enough? For our purpose, anyway," said the chairman.

"I suppose so," said Chiu.

"What *else* is there?"

Chiu shrugged.

"You're right," he agreed.

"And on behalf of the council, I would like to thank you," said the chairman formally.

Chiu smiled gratefully.

"The statement still has to be put to its proper use," he reminded them.

"I don't think we should worry about that, do you?"

"I hope not."

CHAPTER SEVENTEEN

THE WIND WAS STRONGER than the previous day, so the dust from the Gobi drifted in pockets through the capital, gritting the buildings and plants with a light greyish-yellow dust. Charlie saw that a few people wore face masks or pulled scarves up around their mouths. He sat in the Hsin Chiao foyer, cases already packed beside him, knowing he was early but impatient for Chiu's arrival. Because the hotel was organised on the Russian style, with each floor having its own reception staff, the main foyer was remarkably empty. The furniture was frayed and shabby and the walls were patched with quick repair work; it reminded Charlie of a retirement hotel way back from the sea-front at Eastbourne.

The Foreign Office official stopped just inside the entrance when he saw Charlie already waiting.

"I am not late," he said defensively.

"I couldn't sleep," said Charlie truthfully. "So I got up early."

"The car is waiting."

As the vehicle nudged out into the shoals of bicycles, Chiu said: "Fan Yung-ching is still available."

"I have what I came for," said Charlie. "It will be sufficient, believe me."

"It would be difficult to arrange another meeting if anything had been overlooked," warned Chiu.

What were they going to do with the poor old bugger, wondered Charlie.

The car moved out of the Legation district, with its pink-bricked buildings and into the huge T'ien An Men Square.

"There is much to see in Peking," offered Chiu, gesturing towards the red-walled Forbidden City.

"I don't think I've time," said Charlie.

"There is the monument to the Heroes of the Revolution," identified Chiu, pointing through the car window. "The corner-stone was laid by our beloved leader, Mao Tse-tung."

Charlie nodded politely. It reminded him of the Russian statue to their war dead in East Berlin. The department's attempt to kill him, remembered Charlie. He'd actually stood by the Russian statuary and watched the innocent East German he'd cultivated for just such a purpose drive the marked Volkswagen towards the checkpoint. Poor sod had believed he was driving towards an escape to the West.

". . . *How can a man as sensitive as you sometimes be so cruel . . . ?*"

There had been several times Edith had asked him that, unable to understand his peculiar morality of survival. Being Sir Archibald's secretary in the early days, before their marriage, she'd heard it talked about in the department. *Admired* even, as essential for the job. But she hadn't admired it. She'd been frightened of it. He didn't think she had ever been completely sure that it hadn't something to do *with* their marriage: a calculated willingness by Charlie to use her as he seemed willing to use everyone else.

Not even at the very end had she truly believed that it was inherent in him, something of which he was more ashamed than proud.

"You would not care to stop to see the monument?" said Chiu. "Or perhaps the Museum of the Revolution?"

"No thank you," said Charlie. "I'd rather get straight to the airport."

Again the formalities were waived and they were the first on the Canton-bound aircraft. Neither spoke while the other passengers boarded, but as they trundled towards take-off, Chiu said: "You had a good meeting with your embassy?"

Charlie looked at the man beside him. That was the problem, he accepted. He'd never know. Not until it was perhaps too late.

"Very," he said. "The ambassador is making a report to London about your helpfulness."

"It will probably mean fresh application for the man to be returned to Hong Kong."

"Probably," agreed Charlie.

He closed his eyes, hoping the other man would stop forcing the conversation. He was very tired, realised Charlie. But not from the restless, almost unsleeping night. It was an aching mental and physical fatigue, his mind and body stretched against relaxation not just by the need to anticipate the obvious dangers, but to interpret the nuances and half suspicions. He'd swung the pendulum too far, he thought. The rotting inactivity about which he had whined to Willoughby seemed so very attractive now. But wouldn't, he supposed, if he were immersed back into it. Which didn't, at the moment, seem very likely.

He managed to feign sleep until the arrival of the meal.

"We will be in Canton soon," promised Chiu.

And after that, Hong Kong. To what? wondered Charlie.

"I can't thank you enough for the help you've given me," he said sincerely.

"Let us hope it has not been wasted," said Chiu, the criticism obvious.

"Yes," agreed Charlie, unannoyed. "Let's hope."

Because there was special clearance in Canton, they were aboard the express within an hour of touchdown. The same peasants seemed bent beneath the same hats in the same fields, thought Charlie.

"I will keep Mr. Kuo and your Hong Kong legation informed of what happens," promised Charlie.

"What do you intend doing?"

"Lay the information before the Hong Kong police, obviously," said Charlie. "It will be more than sufficient for them to begin enquiries. Then tell our lawyers in London that we have proof upon which they can immediately enter a defence to Lu's claim."

And then flee, he thought.

Chiu nodded. "With no guarantee that there will be either a criminal or civil hearing at which Lu can be denounced."

"It's almost a certainty, in one court or another," said Charlie carelessly.

"*Almost* a certainty," echoed Chiu, throwing the qualification back.

At the border, Chiu escorted him to the bridge.

"Again, my thanks," said Charlie, facing the man near the jostling booth. There appeared more people than when he had entered China, he thought.

"It was in both our interests," said Chiu.

Charlie turned, offering his passport but was again waved through without inspection. He walked across the bridge, glad of the distant sight of a train already in Sheung Shui station. He felt a flush of relief. Then, immediately, annoyance because of it. He had become so nervous that he saw omens of good fortune in something as ridiculous as a waiting train, like a housewife planning her day around a newspaper horoscope. He hadn't realised the strain had become that bad.

He was about a hundred yards into the New Territories when instinct made him react, seconds before the attack became obvious. He swivelled, automatically pulling the overnight bag and briefcase in front of his body as some sort of protection. There were three of them, he saw, marked out against the rest of the

Chinese by their Westernised silk suits. The sort that Lucky Lu favoured, thought Charlie, fleetingly.

They were spaced expertly, so that it would be impossible to confront one without exposing himself to the other two. And approaching unhurriedly, very sure of themselves. The man to the right was even smirking, an expression of anticipation.

Charlie turned to run, but collided at once with an apparently surprised man carrying a jumble of possessions in a knotted rug. It burst open as it hit the ground, cascading pots and pans and clothing, and the man started screeching in bewildered outrage. Charlie tried to dodge around him, brushing off the man's grasping protests, but hit another group who drew together, blocking his escape and gesturing towards the shouting peasant.

He'd never get through, he realised, turning back. The three were still walking calmly and unhurriedly towards him, blocking any dash back to the border. The smiling man had pulled a knife. Narrow-bladed, so there would hardly be any puncture wound. Little risk of identifying blood splashes after the attack. Very professional, judged Charlie.

The peasant was babbling to his left and Charlie swept out, thrusting him aside. The advancing men stopped, warily.

They believed he was seeking space in which to fight, Charlie knew. It wouldn't be a mistake they'd make for longer than a few seconds.

All his life Charlie had existed in an ambiance of violence. But always avoided actual involvement, relying upon mental agility rather than physical ability. A survivor unable to fight his own battles. It was not cowardice, although he was as apprehensive as anyone of physical pain. It was an acceptance of reality. He just wasn't any good at it. Not close up, hand-to-hand brutality. Never had been. No matter how persuasive the lecture or good the instruction, he had never been able to bring himself to complete the motion in training that would, in a proper fight, have maimed or killed. The practise, grown men grunting around a padded floor in canvas suits, had even seemed silly. He'd actually annoyed the instructors by giggling openly.

"One day," Sir Archibald had warned in rare criticism, "there might be the need."

But he'd still been careless. Because the department had had a special section for such activity, men who regarded death or the infliction of pain as a soldier does, uninvolved and detached, a function of their job. He'd only achieved the attitude rarely. To survive, in East Berlin,. And to avenge Edith's murder. And even then it had been remote. He had wanted Edith's killer to die. But not to see the fear of realisation upon his face . . . the sort of fear that the three men could see in him now.

Now there was the need.

They'd started forward again. More confidently. The one with the knife said something and the other two began to grin as well.

They definitely knew, realised Charlie.

"Help!"

He screamed the plea, desperately, instantly aware that other people around had joined in the shouts of the man with whom he had collided, smothering the sound of his voice.

"Help! For Christ's sake, help!"

The crowd pulled away from him and for the briefest moment Charlie thought it was because of his yells. Then he saw it was an almost rehearsed enclave, with the three men facing him just six feet away. And that there were more assailants than he had at first identified.

The handle of his overnight bag was looped with a strap, so that it could be supported on his shoulder. He gripped the top of the strap, whirling it around his head in clumsy arcs, forcing people away from him.

They drew back easily, isolating him in a circle. Twenty at least, decided Charlie. Probably more. No way of knowing.

"The briefcase," demanded the Chinese with the knife. He reached out, beckoning.

Charlie stared back, panting. His eyes locked on the knife in the man's hand. He thought of the pain it would cause thrusting into his body, and his stomach loosened.

"Give me the briefcase," insisted the man. Again he motioned impatiently.

The other two had spaced further out so that he was faced with a wider attack.

The knifeman moved to come forward and again Charlie swept the bag around in a wild, warding-off sweep. Aware that the artificial protests from the peasants had stopped, he screamed again "Help. Please help me!"

He could even see the border in the direction in which he was facing. Less than a hundred yards. The police and officials appeared unaware of what was happening.

It was a cry of shock, not pain, and as he fell Charlie saw that it was one of the long poles from which he'd seen many of the peasants supporting belongings and goods that had been swept across the back of his knees, crumpling his legs beneath him.

The overnight bag hampered him now, the strap becoming entangled with his wrist, and before he could free himself, one of the three men he had first seen had got to him, clamping his arms to his side.

Charlie butted him in the face with his forehead, hearing the grunt of pain. He'd hurt himself, too, he realised, blinking. He tried to scramble up, but felt himself being grabbed behind by unseen hands. Because his eyes were watering, he could only half-focus on the man with the knife. Bending over him. Only feet away.

"I said I wanted the briefcase."

It was a scream of fear this time, with no articulate words.

Charlie thrust back into the people holding him from behind, trying to escape the knife, stomach knotted for the moment of pain. He kicked out, but half bent as he was he missed the man's groin, hitting him harmlessly on the thigh. And then the attacker he'd butted grabbed his leg, twisting him completely over.

Charlie lay face down, sobbing his helplessness. He was almost unaware of the briefcase being snatched from him because of the pain that exploded in his head as something began smashing into his skull, urgent, hammering blows.

But not the pain that he had imagined from the knife, he thought, as he drifted into unconsciousness. Hardly any hurt at all, now that they'd stopped hitting his head.

So death wasn't as painful as he'd always thought it would be.

"Got it!"

Hodgson, who had brought their copy of the Chinese statement into the ambassador's study so the man could refer to it when preparing his report to London, stared down at Collins.

"I'm sorry, sir."

"That man. I knew I'd met him before."

"Oh."

"Prague," declared the ambassador. "Four years ago in Prague."

Hodgson waited, not knowing what was expected of him.

Collins had his eyes closed with the effort of recollection.

"Attached to our intelligence service," he added. "Actually had some sort of altercation with him."

The ambassador opened his eyes, frowning at the memory.

"What's he doing as a director of a Lloyds underwriting firm?" he demanded, as if the young lawyer would have the answer instantly available.

"I don't know," said Hodgson. He hesitated, then risked the impertinence.

"Surely it can't be the same man?" he said.

Collins maintained his distant look.

"Certainly looked like him," he said, his conviction wavering.

"It would take years to attain the seniority that he appeared to have," pointed out Hodgson.

"Quite," conceded Collins, turning back to his desk. "Quite."

CHAPTER EIGHTEEN

HE HADN'T DIED.

The awareness came to him with the first burst of searing pain, as if his head were being crushed between two great weights. He tried to twist, to get the pressure to stop, but that only made it worse and then he heard a sound and realised he was whimpering.

"It'll ache," said a voice. Muzzy. As if the words were coming through cotton wool.

Charlie could feel the strong light against his face and squinted his eyes open carefully, frightened it would cause fresh pain. It did.

There appeared a lot of people standing over him, but his vision was blurred, so he could not distinguish who they were.

"How do you feel?" asked the voice.

"Hurts," managed Charlie. "Hurts like hell."

His voice echoed inside his own head, making him wince.

"We've given him an injection, now we know there's no fracture. It'll get better soon."

Charlie tried focussing again, feeling out with his hands as he did so. A bed. Hospital then.

"Do you feel well enough to talk?"

Another voice: Superintendent Johnson.

Cautiously this time, Charlie turned in the direction of the sound. Still difficult to distinguish the man, but the height was obvious.

"Yes."

"There's a shorthand writer present. He'll record what you say."

"All right."

"Who did it?"

"Chinese."

"Could you recognise them again?"

Charlie considered the question. In his fear, all he'd looked at was the knife. And their clothes. There was the one with the smile: he'd seen his face closely enough.

"Probably," he said.

"Mainland Chinese?"

"They wore Westernised clothing," said Charlie. "Silk suits."

"Did they speak?"

"One did. English."

Whatever drug they'd given him was taking effect. The pain was lessening. And Johnson was becoming easier to see.

"Hong Kong then?"

"It would seem so."

"Why?"

"I'd got the proof."

Charlie blinked at the announcement, wanting very much to see the policeman's face. Johnson was gazing down at him, keeping his face clear.

"Proof?"

"The cook was made available to me in Peking. It was just as the woman said. Everything."

"You brought the statement back?"

"In the briefcase. That was what the man kept saying. He wanted the briefcase."

"When the border guards got to you, you only had a shoulder grip."

"So they got it."

"And the proof?"

Was there almost a sound of relief in Johnson's voice? No, decided Charlie. That was unfair.

"I won't admit I was wrong. Not yet," said Johnson, identifying his attitude.

"I didn't ask you to," said Charlie.

"I'll need more than a statement made by a man to whom I'm refused access. I need facts. So far we haven't even the affidavit you claim was sworn."

Charlie almost shook his head in denial, stopping at the first twinge of warning.

"It was notarised to make it legally admissible by a lawyer from the British embassy," he said. "They have a copy. You could get it from the Foreign Office, in London."

"What did the cook say?"

"That the poison was given to him by John Lu . . . that he'd been told it would only make them ill. And that it would cancel his gambling debt."

"Just as the woman said," repeated Johnson reflectively.

"It will be sufficient to make the enquiries," insisted Charlie.

He could see everything clearly now. Apart from Johnson and the shorthand writer, there was another policeman by the door. Standing near the third officer was a nurse and a white-coated man whom Charlie assumed to be a doctor. They were both Chinese.

"Yes," agreed Johnson. "It will be sufficient to start enquiries. Do you think the Chinese will send the cook back?"

"Definitely not," said Charlie.

"It'll be difficult, trying to proceed on a case like this, with the legal muscle that Lu can employ, with only a sworn statement."

Can you guarantee a court hearing?

The constant demand, from every Chinese official he'd met. Johnson was right, accepted Charlie. And the

Foreign Office statement would only be a copy. Would the company lawyers be prepared to go into court on anything less than the original?

"Yes," said Charlie. "It'll be difficult."

"I'd like a fuller statement later on," said the police chief.

"Of course."

"Maybe tomorrow?"

Johnson put the question more to the doctor than to Charlie.

"Certainly the X rays show there's no fracture," said the white-coated man cautiously. "But there's undoubtedly concussion. I'd like to keep him under observation for a few days."

"Tomorrow," insisted Charlie. There was an uncertainty in his mind, a doubt he could not even formulate. Little more than instinctive caution. But it was there, nagging more intrusively than the pain. And there was something else. The danger of the ambassador's memory. And Jones's curiosity.

"That might not be wise," protested the doctor. "You're lucky not to be more seriously hurt."

"How lucky?"

Charlie put the question to Johnson. The policeman stared back at him curiously.

"What do you mean?" he asked.

"How long was it before the border guards got to me?"

Johnson made an uncertain movement.

"We don't know. They didn't see the beginning of the attack, obviously. By the time they got there, you were unconscious and there wasn't a sign of anyone who'd attacked you."

"Or the briefcase?"

"Or the briefcase," confirmed Johnson.

"One of the men had a knife," said Charlie. "The one who did the talking."

Johnson looked at the doctor.

"Nothing but head injuries," insisted the man. "And minor grazing consistent with being knocked to the ground."

"There was a knife," insisted Charlie. "I saw it."

They didn't understand, he thought.

"So they obviously got the briefcase without having to use it," said Johnson easily. "We can get it all down in the statement."

"I wish you'd give yourself more time," said the doctor.

They thought the knife was an hallucination, decided Charlie.

"I can sign myself out, as I could in England," he demanded.

"Yes," said the doctor.

"I'll agree to stay overnight," promised Charlie. "But tomorrow I'll leave."

It would be ridiculous even to try tonight, he knew. He'd collapse and lengthen the period in hospital.

"You've had at least four severe blows to the head," said the doctor.

"But there's no fracture."

"Concussion can be as bad."

"A night's rest will be sufficient."

"Why don't I call tomorrow?" suggested Johnson, moving to intercede. "To see how you are."

"At the hotel," instructed Charlie.

The doctor's hostility spread to the nurse who remained after everyone else had left. She moved jerkily around the room, showing her irritation in the briskness with which she moved, tidying up after the policemen.

"Would you like a sleeping draught?" she asked finally.

"Please," accepted Charlie. Without help, he knew, he'd never rest.

She returned within minutes with some brown liquid in a tiny medicine glass, waiting by the bedside until he swigged it down.

He relaxed back upon the pillow she plumped for him.

"Good night," she said.

"Good night."

"Something is not right, Charlie," he said to himself after she had left. But what the hell was it?

He began to feel the approach of drowsiness. He turned on the pillow, looking towards the door through which the girl had just left.

Jesus, he thought, as sleep overtook him, I hope that girl is not a gambler.

The ache was still there, but far less than the previous night. Little more than a hangover discomfort. And he'd endured enough of those. The growing belief that he knew what was happening helped. Always the same excitement, the awareness he had realised something that no one else had. He needed more, he accepted. A damned sight more. But at least he had found the direction in which to look for it. At last. And Charlie's Rules, too. Not Judge's.

"I wish you'd stay," said the doctor.

"There are things I must do."

"What?"

"Reports to be made to London, apart from the statement to the police," he said glibly.

"Nothing that couldn't wait."

"I'll be careful," said Charlie. And would have to continue to be, no matter what happened.

The doctor moved his shoulders, abandoning the attempt.

"These might help," he said, handing Charlie a phial of pills. "And if you start vomiting, get back here immediately."

"I will," promised Charlie.

The nurse of the previous day entered, frowning when she saw that Charlie was already dressed.

"Damned glad you don't play Mah jong or follow the horses," greeted Charlie.

The girl stared at him.

"What?" she said.

"Forget it," said Charlie.

"Sure you're all right?" demanded the doctor.

"Positive," insisted Charlie. It had been a bloody silly thing to say. But it had been his first irrational thought upon awakening and from it had come the conclusion that was exciting him.

"You won't change your mind?"

"No."

Charlie walked slowly to the hospital elevator, conscious of the movement against the corridor floor jarring up into his head. There was a slight nausea, deep in his stomach, but he knew it was not from the head wounds. He was actually aware of the customary discomfort from his feet; that had to indicate some improvement.

He reached the hospital reception area and had just realised the need for a car when he heard the shout and turned expectantly.

"Hi there," greeted Harvey Jones.

"Hello," said Charlie. He'd anticipated the approach, but thought it would be back at the hotel. He'd underestimated the man's keenness.

"Heard you got mugged," said the American. "How is it?"

"Still painful," admitted Charlie. "Who told you about the attack?"

"Superintendent Johnson. I've been keeping in touch with him."

"Oh?"

"Thought you might get into contact when you returned from Peking."

"You knew I was there, then?"

"Sure," admitted Jones easily. He motioned towards the forecourt. "I've got a car. Can I give you a lift?"

"Thank you," accepted Charlie.

He relaxed gratefully into the passenger seat, feeling the ache in his body now, as well as his head, and aware how much it had taken from him to travel even this short distance. The doctor had been right. He should have stayed.

"How did you know I'd gone to Peking?" pressed Charlie.

"Kuo Yuan-ching told me."

The American had been easing the car out into the

jammed streets, but he risked a sideways glance to assess Charlie's reaction.

"Quite open about it, was he?"

"Why shouldn't he have been?"

"No reason," agreed Charlie. "Did you try for a visa?"

Again there was a glance from the American, to gauge any sarcasm.

"Yes," he said shortly.

"But he wouldn't give you one?"

"Said it might take months to process. That's why I wanted to know the moment you got back."

"Why?"

"We promised to pool everything we found, remember?"

"I remember," said Charlie. "What have you come up with?"

The car was bogged in traffic and the American turned completely towards Charlie.

"You smart-assing me?" he challenged.

Charlie returned the look, his face open with innocence.

"No," he said. "Why should I?"

The traffic moved and Jones had to look away.

"We're going to work together soon. And you'd better believe it," said the American.

Now it was a blatant threat, recognised Charlie.

"I took a statement from the cook," he said, trying to turn the other man's annoyance.

"And?"

"It confirmed everything we knew but couldn't prove."

"So it wasn't Peking?"

"Definitely not."

"And you've got the statement?"

"That's why I was attacked. The briefcase containing the Chinese original and the signed transcript by a British embassy official were stolen. There was a photograph, too, identifying John Lu."

This time it was Charlie who was studying the American, watching his expression. Jones continued staring straight ahead, moving his fingers lightly against the steering wheel in his impatience with the vehicles around him.

"Lu's men?" demanded Jones finally.

"He'd be the only man to gain by stealing it."

"That's what Superintendent Johnson thinks."

"You must have had quite a discussion with Johnson?"

If Jones had known about the statement and its theft, why had he wanted him to repeat it? Some sort of test, supposed Charlie.

"Johnson's being very helpful," admitted the American.

"Why?"

"I think he believes it's going to be tough to prove anything against Lu, even now . . . and that he's going to need all the assistance he can get."

"And you can provide that assistance?"

Admit it, you bastard, thought Charlie, seizing the opening. You've hinted the Agency might help, in return for favours.

"It's possible," said Jones.

Charlie sat back, letting the discussion go. His headache was worsening. Even though it was difficult without water, he gulped down two of the tablets he had been given at the hospital, coughing when they stuck dryly in his throat.

"Anything wrong?" asked Jones anxiously.

"No," lied Charlie.

They gained the tunnel running beneath the harbour and the car increased its speed. How much had happened in the three weeks since he'd made the same journey with Robert Nelson, reflected Charlie. So many tunnels. So much misunderstanding.

As they emerged, Charlie looked across to the Lu office block.

Guessing Charlie's attention, Jones said: "He'll be worried sick."

"Will he?" said Charlie.

The American laughed at the caution.

"The whole damned thing is about to come down around his ears," he insisted.

"I wish I were as sure," admitted Charlie. "A signed statement was tenuous enough. Now even that's gone."

You're a shit, Charlie, he thought. But he'd never made the pretence of being anything else. Except a survivor. And that's what he was doing now. Surviving. He hoped. Please God that he'd got it right.

Jones eased the car into the edge of Connaught Road and Charlie got out unsteadily in front of the Mandarin Hotel.

"We'll keep in touch," said Jones, leaning across the passenger seat.

"Yes."

"And take care."

"I am," assured Charlie.

CHAPTER NINETEEN

BECAUSE OF THE TIME difference between Hong Kong and London, Superintendent Johnson had been delayed awaiting confirmation that a copy of the Peking statement would be despatched to him as soon as it arrived from China in the diplomatic bag, and so he had only just reached his apartment on the Middle Level when the first contact came from the station inspector.

When he learned it had been an anonymous telephone call to police headquarters, Johnson refused to overrespond. But he listed his instructions carefully, ordering that the forensic and photographic sections should be alerted, in case it were genuine. And that his official car should be sent back.

Then he sat, still in uniform. Waiting.

The second call came within thirty minutes. There was positive confirmation, the duty officer reported. Nothing was being done until his arrival, as he had insisted.

Johnson had been trained at Hendon. And sometimes even here referred to the long-ago lectures and notes. Remembering them now, he sat in the back of the car as it made its way towards Stubbs Road and the Peak, eyes closed, consciously trying to clear his mind of any preconception and suspicion about the fire and the courtroom murders and the claims of a down-at-heel insurance investigator.

He'd need an open mind, he knew. It was going to be a difficult one, the most difficult ever. Particularly now the Foreign Office in London were involved. The sort of thing he tried so hard to avoid. He gripped and ungripped his hands, a frustrated gesture. It was all so damned vague, like imagined shapes in the fog. And the lectures had told him to ignore things that weren't clear. He needed facts. Just plain, straight-forward facts.

He stirred, moved by another thought. Whatever he was driving towards, it certainly seemed that he had been wrong about the fire and the men who had admitted responsibility. Which was going to be bloody embarrassing. Yet the facts had been there, as obvious as the fingers on his hand. Too obvious. And he'd made a mistake. Superintendent Johnson, who was well aware that had he remained in England he would never have risen above the rank of ordinary inspector, didn't like making mistakes. He worried that other people would be made as aware as he was of his limitations and laugh at him.

He nodded with satisfaction at the road block established half a mile from Lu's mansion on Shousan Hill, acknowledging the wave as his recognised car swept through. But it would be the only one allowed past, he was confident. He'd repeated the instruction during the second call. It was the sort of routine at which he was very good.

An inspector was waiting at the already opened gate to Lu's home.

"Well?" demanded Johnson, getting from his car.

"Everything as you asked, sir," said the man. "Nothing done except the servants and guards assembled in one spot so they couldn't interfere with anything."

"How many?"

"Fifteen. John Lu is one of them."

"Yet they heard nothing?"

"Lu apparently relied upon an extensive electrical system."

"So what happened to it?"

"Here," invited the inspector.

Johnson followed the man to a corner of the surrounding wall. It was topped all the way by thick wire mesh.

"Normally enough electricity going through that to kill an elephant," said the inspector.

"What stopped it working?"

With a nightstick, the inspector indicated a corner near brickwork which swept out to begin the imposing entrance through which one had to drive to reach the house.

"There's a conduit box there . . ." he said. He waved an impatient hand and an officer in one of the waiting cars gave him a light operated from the vehicle's battery.

". . . which has been bypassed so that in that corner the wire was turned off. . . ."

In the light of the torch, Johnson could see avoidance leads clamped by their bulldog clips to the live wires and beyond the hole that had been carefully cut through the mesh.

". . . on the other side," said the inspector, "there's the main junction box for this side of the house. Every alarm system has been circuited in the same way."

"An expert?" said Johnson.

"Professional," agreed the officer.

"What about the clips?"

"Haven't let the forensic people get to them until your arrival," said the man. He hesitated.

"But I think you'll find they're of American manufacture and origin," he said, wanting to prove himself.

"American?" demanded Johnson sharply.

The inspector partially retreated at his superior's reaction.

"That's my guess," he said.

"What about the house?"

"It happened in what appears to be the main lounge. I've men guarding it. And an ambulance on the way."

"Ambulance?"

"One of them is still alive."

Johnson waved the inspector towards his car, entered from the other side, and told the driver to go on. Normally, he realised, the grounds would have been floodlit, but the interference with the supply had created an odd, patchwork effect.

The scientific experts were grouped just inside the main entrance to the house. When they saw Johnson's car arrive, they straightened expectantly.

"Give me a moment," he said, moving past them.

He stopped just inside the door of the room the inspector indicated, to get an over-all impression.

"Holy Jesus," he said softly.

It had been a protracted, desperate fight, he decided. A glass-topped table in the middle of the room was splintered and crushed, presumably under the weight of a stumbling body. There were bloodstains, too, which continued to an overturned couch and then led to a wall near the fireplace.

Here all the ornaments and decorations had been swept aside in the struggle, and more blood smeared the walls. A delicate Chinese brushworked painting that had concealed the wall safe hung lopsided, the hook almost torn from the wall. The safe gaped open and inside Johnson had the briefest impression of bundles of money banded together in tight blocks.

But he wasn't interested so much in the safe.

At its foot, his body wedged in a strange awkwardness against the skirting board, lay Harvey Jones. The man's leg was twisted beneath him; he'd broken it when he fell, thought Johnson, his mind registering the details with a clinical, later-to-be-produced-in-court accuracy.

Near the man's outstretched left hand was a tall pedestal ornament, its heavy base messily bloodstained. There was a matching ornament on the other side of the fireplace, Johnson saw, cracked where it had fallen to the ground.

He knelt to get closer to the body. Jones's eyes were still open, in a shocked expression of death, and the police chief could just see the bullet entries. One, high in the left shoulder, was little more than a flesh wound, but there was another, lower in the chest. And from the amount of blood it was clear there was a third that he couldn't immediately see.

Johnson had begun to straighten before he saw the document. He crouched again, trying to read it without displacing it before the photographs were taken. There was a slight splash of blood on one corner. And the man's arm obscured the beginning. But it was quite easy for Johnson to read at least a third and identify the signature of Geoffrey Hodgson alongside the seal of the British embassy in Peking.

He stood slowly. So, he wouldn't have to await the arrival of the diplomatic bag.

"Here," called the inspector.

The Chinese millionaire was crumpled so that he was almost completely concealed by the desk. From the man was coming the snorted breathing of someone deeply unconscious, and by moving around behind him, Johnson could see that there was a deep triangular gash at the side of Lu's head.

The police chief looked across at the ornament by Jones's outstretched hand. The base could have created just such a wound.

Facts, he recognised, contentedly. Presentable, unarguable facts. Soon it would be time to bring the photographers and scientists in, to commence the simple, logical routine.

"Quite a fight," suggested the inspector.

Drawers had been jerked from their runners and in two places Johnson could see where the locks had been forced, crudely jemmied open by some strong leverage. The contents were strewn over the desk haphazardly, as if someone had been looking for something particular and discarded what he didn't want, without care where it landed.

Again Johnson crouched, grunting with the difficulty of getting his large body beneath the narrow leg-space of the desk. About six inches from Lu's right hand lay a pistol. Johnson lowered himself to it, sniffing, immediately twitching his nose at the smell of cordite.

"Czech," identified the inspector. "M-27."

"Rough-looking weapon," said Johnson, rising.

"But able to be fitted with a silencer," said the inspector, indicating the attachment.

There was movement at the door and Johnson turned.

"The ambulance is here," reported the guarding policeman.

"Let them come in," said Johnson. "And forensic and photographic, too."

The experts entered in a bunch.

"Photographs first," stipulated Johnson, sure of his case and therefore sure of himself.

The white-coated ambulance men entered with their stretcher.

"The man's here," said Johnson. "But before he's moved I want a paraffin test on his hands, to establish that he's recently fired a gun."

Immediately one of the plainclothes men opened a bag and began walking towards the desk.

"Superintendent Johnson."

The police chief turned at the inspector's summons.

"This would seem to be the point of entry," said the officer.

A neat semicircle had been cut from the glass near the interior catch of the ceiling-to-floor window.

"That's it," agreed Johnson.

"Not difficult to see what happened?"

"Quite obvious," agreed Johnson. "Intruder, surprised by the householder in the middle of a robbery, is shot but manages to bludgeon the man to the ground but dies of his injuries as he tries to retrieve from the safe what he's looking for."

"Looking for?"

"Something I thought was going to create the most difficult case I'd ever been called upon to handle," admitted the police chief. "But now it looks like one of the easiest."

The inspector pointed towards the dead man at the far side of the room.

"Quite an expert, wasn't he?"

"Oh, he was an expert right enough," said Johnson.

The inspector turned at the confidence in his superior's voice.

"Did you know him?"

Johnson smiled.

"He worked for the American government," he disclosed. "The Central Intelligence Agency."

"Oh," said the inspector doubtfully. "That could cause some problems, couldn't it?"

"I don't see why," said Johnson.

The facts were there after all. No one could argue with that. Plain as the fingers on his hand.

Charlie Muffin was finally sick. He stood sweating over the lavatory bowl, agonised by the head pain that came with each stomach-stretching retch. When he could finally leave the bathroom it was difficult to see, and for a moment, he thought he was suffering from the double vision with which he'd awakened in hospital.

He sat quietly on the edge of the bed, blinking the wetness from his eyes. He was limp with perspiration. And smelt. Like the confused old man in the Peking interview room.

Charlie reached out for the pills the doctor had given him, concerned at how few remained in the bottle. It would be sensible to go back to hospital. Sensible. But impossible.

He undressed carelessly, leaving his clothes puddled on the floor. He didn't bother to get beneath the bed covering, because he knew he wouldn't sleep.

It was going to be a long time until the morning, he thought.

CHAPTER TWENTY

JOHNSON TOOK the document from Charlie, nodding with satisfaction at another established fact.

"No doubt at all?"

"No," said Charlie. "That's definitely the statement I took from the cook in Peking."

"And the one that was stolen from you at the border?"

"Yes."

"And this is the photograph, identifying John Lu?" Yes."

The police chief sat back expansively. "That's it then. Everything explained."

"It would seem so," agreed Charlie. There was no pain now, but if he moved his head quickly he still felt a slight dizziness. It had all been brilliantly conceived, he thought. Which meant he was still in great danger.

". . . *You'll always have to run, Charlie . . . always. . . .*"

"Be a defence to the killing, of course," said Johnson. "Reduced to manslaughter or even, with a good counsel, justifiable homicide in the protection of his property."

"Yes."

"In fact Jones's killing is unimportant compared to the door it opened."

The fitting epitaph, thought Charlie sadly. "Here lies Harvey Jones, whose death served a purpose."

"It would seem I owe you an apology," conceded Johnson unexpectedly. "You were right."

"It would have been difficult to prove," Charlie admitted, indicating the statement. "Even with that."

"But not now," said the police chief.

"No," said Charlie. "Not now. What about John Lu?"

"The widest open door of them all."

"What do you mean?"

"He was among those detained at the house last night. So he couldn't run. And he panicked. Started making admissions before we even asked the questions."

"You were lucky."

"Luckier than we thought. His lawyers are trying to do a deal now, to salvage something of the mess into which he talked himself."

"What sort of deal?"

"His evidence against his father, together with all the details of the crime empire, in exchange for a guarantee against prosecution."

"Not very Chinese, son turning against father, is it?"

Johnson laughed. The policeman was very happy with himself, thought Charlie.

"I told you not to take any notice of that folklore rubbish," he said.

"Yes," said Charlie. "You told me. Will you accept his offer?"

"Make an unbreakable case," defended Johnson.

The policeman sat forward as the thought came to him.

"And it would be the end of any claim against you, if he'd agree to be a witness."

"Yes," said Charlie. "It would."

"He hated his father, apparently," said Johnson.

"Hated him?"

"Always. Have you told your people in London?"

Charlie nodded.

"I telephoned before coming here," he said. Willoughby had almost sobbed with relief.

"It'll be a hell of a case when it finally comes to court."

"Yes," said Charlie. Johnson saw a lot of personal credit coming from it.

"And not just because of Lu and who he is," continued Johnson. "You didn't have any idea that Jones was an American intelligence agent, did you?"

"No," said Charlie. "No idea at all."

"He was," confided Johnson. "There's an enormous diplomatic flap."

"I suppose there would be," said Charlie. He looked at his watch.

"Coming to the remand hearing?" invited Johnson.

"Yes," said Charlie, rising.

It was difficult to keep in step with the large man, and Charlie's head began to hurt again.

"I wondered if you would do me a favour," he said.

Johnson slowed, looking sidways. "Of course."

Now the man was almost overcompensating in his friendliness, thought Charlie.

"I want to find the woman," said Charlie.

"Woman?"

"Jenny Lin Lee, the woman who was with Nelson."

Johnson stopped completely, turning across the corridor towards Charlie.

"She's not at Nelson's flat any longer," explained Charlie.

"You think she's gone back whoring?"

Charlie knew he would never be able to think of that word as anything but offensive and ugly.

"Yes," he said.

"Shouldn't be too difficult," promised Johnson, setting off towards the court again. "Call me tomorrow."

"I will," said Charlie. "Early."

He'd already booked his return flight to London. He

was taking a risk even now. But there were other things to do.

It was the same court as that in which the two Chinese shipyard workers had appeared, and again there was a crush for admission. Because he was with Johnson, Charlie entered ahead of everyone else, with a choice of seats.

"I gather Lu is flying lawyers from London when the case opens," said Johnson.

"When will that be?"

"I shall apply for remands until we reach a decision with the son. But it shouldn't take too long. I've got an unarguable case."

Just as he had with the fire and the poor sods who'd got killed, thought Charlie. How was it that people like Johnson got into positions of power? There was a great similarity between the police chief and the people who'd taken over the department after Sir Archibald's death.

"Unarguable," agreed Charlie.

Johnson identified the sarcasm.

"Surely you don't think this is wrong?" he demanded.

Charlie hesitated, avoiding an immediate reply.

"You've got a good case," he said finally.

The ushers began to admit the public and Charlie moved away, towards the seat he had occupied when he and Nelson had been in court.

He turned at Lu's entry into the court. The millionaire's head was turbanned with bandages, and a medical attendant was in the back of the dock, as well as the warders. Lu stared defiantly towards the magistrates' bench, hand gripping the top of the dock.

The court rose for the magistrates' entry and immediately the clerk read out the charge of murder against Lu.

Johnson rose, as the man finished.

"I would make a formal application for a week's remand," he said officiously. "At which time I anticipate the police being in a position to indicate when they could proceed."

172 The Inscrutable Charlie Muffin

The local solicitor representing Lu until the arrival
of the London counsel hurried to his feet. He was
wearing an Eton tie, Charlie saw.

"I would like it entered into the court records at this
first hearing that my client utterly denies the preposterous charge against him," said the man. "Were it based
on fact, there would be a producible defence against it.
But it is not. I would therefore make application for
bail, asking the court to consider my client's position in
this community. He would, of course, be prepared to
surrender his passport."

"Having regard to the seriousness of the charge, together with other matters still under investigation, the
police oppose bail most strongly," objected Johnson instantly.

"Bail refused," declared the magistrate chairman.

As the solicitor moved to speak, the man went on:
"You have the right, of course, to apply to a Judge in
chambers."

"An application will be made," insisted the solicitor.

"He won't get it," Johnson said to Charlie, as the
court cleared.

"No," said Charlie, disinterested. It was almost time
for his appointment.

"Know what the defence is going to be?"

Charlie paused at the court exit, turning back to the
police chief.

"What?"

"That he knows nothing whatever about what happened to Harvey Jones. . . ."

Johnson laughed, inviting Charlie's reaction.

When Charlie said nothing, Johnson added: "Ridiculous, isn't it?"

"Yes," agreed Charlie. "Ridiculous."

"No risk at all?"

Willoughby nodded at his wife's question.

"No risk at all. Not any longer."

She came towards him, arms outstretched.

"Why darling, that's wonderful."

He refused to bend towards her, and because of his height, she wasn't able to pull herself up to kiss him.

"Oh," she said. "Punishment?"

"What did you expect?"

"There's no need to be . . . to be . . ." she stumbled.

". . . uncivilised?" he offered.

"Or sarcastic."

He closed his eyes helplessly. Why couldn't he just tell her to get out? She'd been going, after all.

"Do you still want me to leave?"

"You know the answer to that."

"Do you still want me to leave?" she persisted.

"No," he conceded, his voice a whisper.

"Then you mustn't be cruel to me."

"You're a cow," he said.

"Which is a very rude and offensive word. But I've never pretended to be otherwise."

The usual defence, he thought.

"What about this man who's done it all . . . ?"

". . . Charlie?"

"Charlie! What a delightfully coarse name! *Is* he coarse, darling?"

"Strange, in many ways," allowed Willoughby.

"I simply *must* meet him."

"Yes," agreed the underwriter. "You must."

"Very soon."

"All right. Very soon."

"Rupert."

"What?"

"Say you love me."

"I love you."

CHAPTER TWENTY-ONE

KUO YUAN-CHING LOOKED cautiously across the desk, head to one side in what Charlie had come to realise as an habitual pose.

"I'm intrigued at your visit," said the Chinese.

"You shouldn't be," said Charlie. It would be wrong to let this man imagine any superiority.

Kuo let an expression reach his face, but refused to respond directly to the remark. Instead he said: "Everything would seem to have been resolved far better than you had hoped."

"And you'll get your court denunciation."

"It would seem likely," admitted Kuo.

"It's inevitable," predicted Charlie. "Especially now that John Lu wants to save himself by turning Queen's evidence."

"Then we're both satisfied."

"No," said Charlie. "I'm not satisfied at all."

"Not having saved £6,000,000!"

"That's not what I meant."

"What then?"

"I know what happened," announced Charlie.

Kuo remained expressionless, hands resting lightly on the tabletop.

"Doesn't everybody?" he said.

"No, Mr. Kuo. Hardly anybody."

The man shook his head, raising his hands in a gesture of bewilderment.

"You baffle me," he protested condescendingly.

"For a long time, you baffled me," said Charlie. "And then I thought of the incredible help and all the conern about Lu being publicly denounced. And then I remembered what Mr. Chiu told me, as we were going to Peking."

"What was that?"

" 'People who bring disgrace to China never go unpunished,' " quoted Charlie.

Kuo nodded seriously.

"That's true," he agreed. "We're sometimes a vindictive nation."

"I've often been accused of the same fault. Perhaps that's how I finally realised the truth."

"Is vindictiveness necessarily a fault?"

"It's taken me a long time to recognise it," admitted Charlie. Too long, he thought.

"I'm still waiting to be surprised," prompted Kuo.

". . . Apart from the fact that I should have been wounded by the knife, the border attack was very convincing . . . even to the suits your people wore. Just like Lu's men. But not to use the knife was a mistake. . . ."

"Our people!" echoed Kuo.

"Your people," insisted Charlie. "No one except the Chinese authorities knew when I would be returning across the border with the statement involving Lu. So it couldn't have been anyone else, could it?"

There was a disparaging expression upon Kuo's face.

"But why should we steal from you an affidavit we went to such enormous trouble to ensure you obtained!" he said.

"To guarantee, even if it meant murder, the public disgrace of Lu," said Charlie positively. "A disgrace that I *couldn't* guarantee, not even with the statement."

"A very wild flight of fancy," said Kuo mildly.

"No," argued Charlie. "Not wild at all. Just a sensible interpretation of Peking's determination to maintain its rapport with America . . . a rapport important enough to risk the death of an American agent . . . an agent whom you took particular care to let know the facilities I'd been given and who you knew would make an effort to retrieve incriminating evidence if enough people pointed him to it. And enough people did. . . ."

Charlie paused.

". . . Which was why I wasn't knifed," he accepted. "I had to set the bait, didn't I?"

Kuo pushed his chair slightly away from the table, making a small grating sound.

"It actually removed the risk of having to snatch him off the streets, with all the problems of failure that that might have created, didn't it? All you had to do was follow him until he got to Lu's house . . . ?"

"People who know more about it than me said you were extremely clever, Mr. Muffin," said Kuo conversationally. "But I don't think any of us believed you'd work it out as far as you have. You really are a surprising man."

Charlie sat motionless, numbed by the identification.

"Why bewilderment, Mr. Muffin? You'd expect Peking to have extensive files on all American and British operatives, wouldn't you?" said Kuo, still casual. "Just like they have about our people."

Charlie still couldn't respond.

"It was little more than a routine cross-reference with your picture, almost as soon as you arrived in the colony to question the fire, that gave us your identity," said the Chinese.

The Chinese had assumed control, decided Charlie.

"And you were right," continued Kuo. "We had far more reason than any British insurance company to expose Lu. So nothing could be left to chance."

The almost constant impression of surveillance, remembered Charlie. So his instinct wasn't failing. He

felt the relief of a man fearing blindness being assured
that all he needed was reading glasses.

"Your coming really fascinated us," admitted Kuo.
"Particularly as your file had you marked as dead."

He leaned forward across the desk.

"And such an interesting file," he said. "We could
easily appreciate why London and Washington would
want you killed."

Russia would have leaked the humiliation of the
British and the Americans, Charlie knew; they'd seen it
from the beginning as a propaganda coup. He was not
surprised that Peking knew the details.

"You made very full use of me, didn't you?" he said
at last.

"As much as we possibly could," conceded Kuo.
"The arrival of the man Jones made it perfect for us."

"Otherwise mine would have been the body found in
Lu's lounge?"

Kuo's face opened with the obviousness of the answer.

"It would have had to have been someone, wouldn't
it?" he said. "And you would have had as much reason
to try to retrieve the document as the American. More,
maybe."

"But I'm not being able to escape, am I?" guessed
Charlie.

"Escape?"

"Within twenty-four hours this colony will be inun-
dated with men from Washington, investigating the
death of one of their operatives," predicted Charlie.
"To point them towards me would round the whole
thing off very neatly, wouldn't it?"

"You're a very suspicious person, Mr. Muffin."

"I have to be."

Kuo nodded.

"Yes," he agreed. "Of course."

"Do you intend exposing me?" demanded Charlie.

Kuo sighed, a man facing an unpleasant duty.

"It's very unlikely that they'd see the flaw you recognised. No one was as completely involved as you, after

all. But there's always the outside possibility. And as I've said, we can't leave anything to chance."

"So to be handed me might deflect their curiosity?"

"You must admit," said Kuo, "Washington would be very interested."

Moving slowly, so the man would not misunderstand, Charlie put his hand into the inside pocket of his jacket and took out an envelope.

"As interested, perhaps, as they would be in these?" he said.

Kuo's control was very good, thought Charlie. There was not the slightest indication of emotion as the man went carefully through the photographs.

The first showed quite clearly Harvey Jones bypassing the alarms at Lu's house. There were more, of Chinese this time, at the same spot at the wall. The pictures of the American's apparently unconscious body being bundled into the lounge was slightly blurred, because of the distance from which it had been taken, but still recognisable as the man. There were several pictures of a car, with the number plate clearly identifiable.

"The registration would prove it to be the vehicle assigned to this legation, wouldn't it?" asked Charlie.

"Oh yes," agreed Kuo. He looked up. "Infra-red photography?"

"I was professionally trained," said Charlie. "I actually entered the department because of it."

"They're very good," said Kuo, as if he were admiring holiday snapshots.

"The only difficulty is the need to keep the film refrigerated until just before use and then getting it developed as soon as possible afterwards," said Charlie. "Fortunately in a place like Hong Kong I had no difficulty buying a 0.95 lens."

"The negatives and more prints are obviously in a safe place?" said Kuo, bored with the phoney civility.

"Obviously," agreed Charlie, unworried by the threat. He looked at his watch.

"One set will almost be in London by now," he said.

He was back in an environment he believed he'd left forever. He felt very much at home.

"With a complete account?" queried Kuo.

"Very full," confirmed Charlie.

"You could have saved Jones," accused the Chinese suddenly.

"I tried," said Charlie. But only after he had guaranteed his own survival.

"The telephone call to the police?"

Charlie nodded.

"But I was too late," he said. As always.

"I wondered about the call," said Kuo. "It was much sooner than that which we had planned to make. We were almost caught."

"I know," said Charlie, taking another picture from his pocket.

Kuo was shown twice by the identifiable car.

"Really very clever," praised the man.

"As I said, I have to be."

"Just as I had to be there," said the Chinese, in explanation. "We realised the risk, of course. But I had to see the affidavit was put in the right place. And guarantee the little, important things . . . like ensuring the firing traces would be found on Lu's right and not left hand. . . ."

"Nothing could be left to chance," remembered Charlie.

"Exactly."

"Keep the photographs," offered Charlie. "I expect you'll want other people to see them. Mr. Chiu, for instance."

Kuo nodded, putting them into a drawer in the desk.

"I congratulate you," said Kuo.

He didn't feel any pride, realised Charlie. Just relief. And regret. The regret of which Edith had never thought him capable.

"It would seem," said Kuo, "that we will part in friendship."

"Not exactly friendship," qualified Charlie. "More in complete understanding."

Kuo smiled.

"It's been an interesting experience, Mr. Muffin."

"For both of us," agreed Charlie.

Johnson had wanted to send someone with him, but Charlie had refused the protection.

The shack was actually against the Kowloon waterfront, part of the tin-drum and cardboard shanty town to the east of the city.

Charlie felt the attention as soon as he entered, stopping just inside the door to adjust to the darkness. And not just attention, he realised. Hostility, too.

The mutter of conversation began again, but everyone was still watching him, he knew. Everyone except Jenny. She was at the bar, head bent in apparent interest in something before her.

He picked his way through the trestles at which the Chinese sat, careful not to come into contact. It would need little excuse for an argument to erupt, he decided.

As he got near to the girl, he saw the hair of which she had once been so proud was greased with dirt and matted in disorder.

"Jenny," he said quietly.

Her glass was almost empty. She was staring down into it intently, but her eyes were fogged and unseeing.

"Jenny," he tried again.

The barman positioned himself in front of him.

"Beer," said Charlie.

The man looked at the girl and Charlie nodded. There was still no reaction when her glass was refilled.

He reached out, touching her arm. She was very cold, despite the ovenlike heat of the place. She responded at last to his touch, squinting sideways. There was no immediate recognition.

"Twenty dollars," she said distantly. "Very good for twenty dollars."

"Jenny," he said again, trying to reach her.

". . . Hong Kong, not American," she recited automatically. "Fuck all night. Just twenty dollars."

There were no puncture marks on her arms. He

looked down and saw the needle bruises around her ankles, near the big vein.

"Know you," she said thickly.

The cheongsam was the one she had worn the night she had come to his room. It was very stained, and the thigh split had been torn so that it gaped almost to her groin.

"Came to fire Robert."

She smiled with the pride of a child remembering a difficult multiplication table.

"Lu lost," said Charlie. "Too many other people did, as well. But Lu lost."

There was no comprehension.

"Robert came here," she said, mouthing the words slowly. "That night. He came here."

He reached out again, trying physically to squeeze some reaction from her.

"Lu has been arrested," he said.

". . . very brave, coming here by himself. Round-eyes aren't allowed . . . now they've made me come here . . . work here . . . punishment. . . ."

Charlie lodged against the barstool, looking at her sadly. The heroin had almost completely blanketed her mind. She would take months to cure. Months of patient, constant care. He looked at his watch. The flights that would be bringing in the American investigation teams to supplement those already in the colony would be arriving within three hours.

It would have to be someone else.

She blinked her eyes, as if remembering something.

"All night," she said. "Only twenty dollars. Anything you want."

She snatched out, suddenly desperate when she saw him move.

"Fifteen then. Anything you want for fifteen."

He shrugged her hand away, threading between the unsteady tables again. It didn't matter if he collided with anybody, he realised. They had wanted him to find her and see what had happened.

"Bastard," she screamed behind him. "Fired Robert."

Yes, thought Charlie, stepping unsteadily out into the street. He was a bastard. Literally. And in every other way. Usually he wasn't as ashamed of it as he was now. She wouldn't have understood had he tried to explain he wasn't abandoning her.

CHAPTER TWENTY-TWO

WILLOUGHBY NEEDED movement to let off his excitement, striding without direction about the room. For the first time he was holding himself upright, Charlie saw. He really was remarkably tall.

"Unbelievable," said the underwriter, groping for words sufficient to express himself. "A miracle . . . nothing short of a miracle. . . ."

The grandfather clock in the corner of Willoughby's office chimed the half-hour and Charlie looked across to it. Still another hour before the appointment. The chiropodist would probably insist upon the supports being put into his shoes. Mean another pair, he supposed. Wonder how difficult it would be, adjusting to an artificial lump beneath each foot?

"People got hurt," reminded Charlie, puncturing the other man's euphoria. "Too many people."

Willoughby stopped the pacing, looking seriously at Charlie.

"And not just in Hong Kong," he said obscurely.

"I don't understand," said Charlie. Despite the chiropodist, he could still get to Guildford before the rush hour. He hoped Edith's grave hadn't become too neglected.

Willoughby shook himself like a dog throwing off water.

"It's not important," he dismissed. "Incidentally, there was quite a lot of money due to Robert Nelson. . . . I sent it to our new broker. . . ."

"There was a woman," said Charlie hopefully. "It's important to arrange something for her. . . ."

"Jenny Lin Lee?" interrupted Willoughby.

Charlie nodded.

"She's dead."

"Oh."

"Massive drug overdose, apparently," said the underwriter. "The police have decided it was self-administered, so there's no question of any crime."

Already stencilled "closed" and filed in one of Johnson's neat little cabinets by one of his neat little clerks, thought Charlie. Again he'd been too late.

"She knew Lu would win some sort of victory," said Charlie softly.

"What?"

"Nothing," said Charlie.

"I'll always be indebted to you," declared the underwriter, sitting at last at his desk.

"It took me a long time to realise how long I'd been away," said Charlie. "Almost too long."

He would never know about the Peking ambassador, he thought. Not until it was too late, anyway.

"I wouldn't like it to end," said Willoughby. "In fact, Clarissa wants to meet you."

"Clarissa?"

"My wife. Let's meet socially, very soon."

"Thank you."

"I'm sorry for the way all this began, Charlie. It was wrong to treat you as I did."

"Forget it."

"I'd like the association to continue."

Charlie shifted uncertainly. How soon would it be before the fear diminished and the boredom began eating away at him again?

"I don't know," he said. "I made a lot of mistakes."

"But won in the end."

"Only just."

Which was all he could ever hope for, decided Charlie. To win. By a small margin.

Ed McBain's Classic

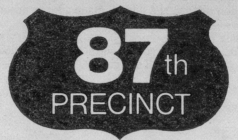

87th PRECINCT

Mysteries...

"The best of today's police stories...lively, inventive, and wholly satisfactory." *The New York Times*